HOW I FOUND THE STRONG

✦ HOW I FOUND THE ✦

STRONG

A CIVIL WAR STORY
by Margaret McMullan

 HOUGHTON MIFFLIN COMPANY BOSTON 2004

ACKNOWLEDGMENTS

I would like to thank my father, James McMullan; the Center for the Study of Southern Culture at the University of Mississippi; the Smith County Courthouse in Raleigh, Mississippi; and Ernest Russell for all the research assistance. I would also like to thank my friends, family, and colleagues for their genuine interest in this material, and the University of Evansville for providing me with a generous research grant. Most especially, my thanks goes to Frank Russell for passing down *his* story.

Very special thanks must also go to my husband, Patrick O'Connor. And finally, I must send many thanks to my agent, Jennie Dunham, my editor, Margaret Raymo, my copyeditor, Albert LaFarge, and all the wonderful people at Houghton Mifflin.

www.houghtonmifflinbooks.com

The text of this book is set in 11.5-point Bulmer

Library of Congress Cataloging-in-Publication Data
McMullan, Margaret.
How I found the Strong / by Margaret McMullan.
p. cm.
Summary: Frank Russell, known as Shanks, wishes he could have gone with his father and brother to fight for Mississippi and the Confederacy, but his experiences with the war and his changing relationship with the family slave, Buck, change his thinking.
ISBN 0-618-35008-x
1. Mississippi—History—Civil War, 1861–1865—Juvenile fiction. [1. Mississippi—History—Civil War, 1861–1865—Fiction. 2. United States—History—Civil War, 1861–1865—Fiction. 3. Family life—Mississippi—Fiction. 4. Slavery—Fiction.] I. Title.
PZ7.M478915HO 2004   [Fic]—dc22   2003012294

Manufactured in the United States of America
VB 10 9 8 7 6 5 4 3 2 1

For my father, James
&
For my son, James

Spring 1861

IN THE EARLY MORNING the day of the barbecue, laurel and Indian pipe bloom in the woods. Ma sweeps the porch, saying how it's too pretty out for a war. She calls me in from the henhouse to help load up the wagon. The men finish planting the fields while I let out the chickens and the cow, shovel the stalls, and spread clean straw.

In the kitchen, Grandma cards cotton while Grandpa still sleeps in the feather bed in the front room. Grandma lost her sight to old age four years ago, but she says she doesn't need her eyes to card cotton. There's a basket of clean white cotton on one side of her, and on the other is a basket of uncarded cotton dappled with seeds and dirt.

"Shanks," she says. "Light my pipe, Sonny."

Seems like I'm always filling Grandma's corncob pipe with more tobacco, and I hate this. I don't like the smell or the feel of the dry leaves, I don't like it when Grandma calls me Sonny, but most of all, I don't like it when she runs her cold, bony fingers over my face and neck, even over my shoulders and arms.

"You still a skinny boy, aren't you?" she says. "Nothin' but a beanpole."

She goes on and on about how I should be a preacher, and I can hardly stand to hear any of it again because everybody knows that only sissies are preachers—boys who can't do nothing else but read and write.

The house smells of the maypop jelly Ma is making. Ma is bent over the kettle, laughing at what Grandma has to say about me, and having herself a taste test. She opens the back door and the room is filled with light and a wild-onion breeze. She kisses me on the neck and I can almost taste the sticky cooked sugar on her breath.

Abraham Lincoln has just declared war on us. Yesterday we collected more blackberries and maypops than we ever have in all our lives. I am ten. My brother Henry is fourteen, old enough to be a soldier. If I were two years older I could be a drummer boy.

Ma and me load up the wagon with food, canteens, and bandages. I watch Pa, Henry, and Buck break from the work under the shade of the tree that is shaped like a Y. Before Grandma lost her sight, she told me Henry was Pa's favorite because he looks so much like Pa. They're both big-shouldered and ruddy-skinned. With my fair hair, I take after Ma. I can see Pa's lips moving and Henry looking all serious. They are talking strategy and survival, and I wish just for once I could be in on their conversating. Every night, Henry and Pa sit together on the porch, cleaning their rifles, sharpening their bayonets, and talking about the war. And every night, I can't help but wish I was the older brother going off to war with Pa.

Pa even likes our Negro, Buck, more than he likes me, because Buck is so strong you don't even notice it. When you ask Buck to lift, he lifts. Say chop, he chops. And how strong is Henry? One year, Pa won a wood chopping contest at the fair, and the next year Henry matched Pa's record just to prove he was as strong.

Even though they are hot and tired from planting corn

all morning, I see Pa smile at something Henry says, and nobody seems to mind that Buck leans his head back against the trunk of the tree and closes his eyes. In that light, Buck's skin looks like wet blue paint.

I seen Pa whip Buck once. Pa says he owns Buck and he has a right to expect work from him. When Buck doesn't work, Pa has to punish him, same as he does with Henry. Henry is not as big as Buck, but he eats more than anybody I've seen, and he never cries when Pa takes him out to the back of the henhouse and whips him with a hickory switch. Pa has never come close enough to me to whip me.

"Tributary to the Pearl River up ahead. Pearl runs into the Strong." Pa always says this when we get to the unnamed stream a few miles south of our place. Buck's shoulders stiffen as he walks toward the water.

"Where *is* the Strong, Pa?" I ask.

"About thirty miles from where you're sittin'. It runs west of Smith, through Simpson County, Mississippi. Go on, Buck, you're all right," Pa yells out from the wagon. "If you want barbecue, we have to ford this here river."

Buck keeps on walking toward the riverbank; then he stops. He just freezes, like his feet won't go nowhere.

Pa laughs, then gets down from the wagon. Without a word between them, Pa takes the reins Buck's been holding and Buck mounts our mule named Ben. In the wagon, Ma reads her Bible while Grandma cards cotton, making as much noise as she can near Grandpa's sleeping head. Henry sits next to me on the tailgate of the wagon and cleans his rifle, and I don't do nothing but swing my legs off the back while Pa leads us all across the river.

"You ever look at Buck? He never looks too well satisfied," Henry says, looking up from the barrel of his rifle.

"That's just Buck's way," I say.

"You ever seen Buck smile?"

I poke my head around the back of the wagon. Buck rides Ben, staring straight ahead, careful not to look down at the water that is swirling around the mule's tendony legs. Buck keeps his kinked hair cut short, and I can see one side of his face, his jaw muscles working. What with all the talk of slavery, seems like I start to take notice of Buck for the first time, even though we grew up together. I have not thought of Buck as property before all this business with secession and the war, but then again I have not thought much of Buck at all before. None of us here in Smith County think much about the colored folk living amongst us. They are like the tables and chairs we sit on and eat from. They are just there.

I sit back down next to Henry. "He sure ain't smiling now," I say.

"Course not. There's water."

After a good bit, Henry says the war doesn't have anything to do with slavery. The Yankees just want our land and ports. They want to break us because we're getting stronger than them. I can tell by the way Henry's talking that he's got his teeth clenched the way Pa does when he's mad.

When Pa gets back into the wagon, I have to ask: "Why do you 'spec Buck's so fearful of water?"

"Some folks are scared of fire, some of being buried alive," Pa says. "Buck was just a kid when him and his mama come up on a flatboat on the Mississippi. There was a terrible storm, and I 'magine Buck recalls seeing his mama drown."

I think about how dark and muddy the water must have been, and how you probably couldn't see the river from the rain. Pa bought Buck in Mobile. I don't know what happened to Buck's pa, or if he has any sisters or brothers.

"They can't swim, you know," Grandma says, smelling like lady powder and tobacco. "None of the colored peoples can."

The wagon jumps and Grandpa sits up, wide-eyed and finally awake.

Most everybody in the county is at the barbecue at Liberty Church. Pa and Henry join the other men in line to get their new uniforms, and then they drill. They were amongst the first to join up. Last year, Mississippi was the second state to secede, which Pa is not so proud of because, he says, we should have been the first.

Grandma and Ma spread a cloth on the ground and set out food. Grandpa starts playing his harmonica.

"Hush that devil music," Grandma says. Already she's pulling out the cotton balls she keeps in her pocket for carding. She grumbles for her pipe. "Shanks? Sonny? Come light yer poor ol' grandma's pipe."

My *name* is *Frank*, I want to say. Frank Russell. Pa may call me Shanks on account of my skinny legs, but it's not Sonny and it's not Chicken Legs and it's not Beanpole. It's Frank.

"Heya, Shanks." Sheriff Matkin tousles my hair, then takes off his hat as he greets Ma and Grandma. He laughs when he sees Grandma carding cotton.

"Don't you know about cotton gins, Mrs. Russell?"

"I got my own old way of doing things," Grandma says without stopping her carding and without breaking a smile.

Sheriff Matkin nods to Grandpa.

"Still time to join up."

"Ain't my war," Grandpa says and sets to blowing into his harmonica again. Grandma winces.

I stand beside Ma, who is wearing a hoop skirt made from whalebone that Pa bought for her in Mobile for $1.85. Ma hardly ever wears hoop skirts. She can hardly sit down. The hoops chink together as she walks and moves, and the dress is so wide I feel miles from her.

Yards from us, Mr. McCollum is already showing all the ladies his white linen trousers from Scotland. He looks like a sausage ready to pop, but he invites the women, especially the young ones, to get a closer look at the fine horn buttons on the side.

The two militia companies come marching into the churchyard, with their drums and fifes and fiddles playing and flags waving. The soldiers are wearing their kepi hats, their new gray uniforms with the brass buttons, and the shoes that Mr. Childre made for them—brogans that he cut for the right and the left foot. Each separate. Neither Pa nor any of the other men in Smith County have thought to do this before. Some of the men wear sabers that get in their way as they walk.

I have never seen the Confederate flags. One has three thick stripes and a circle of stars, the other is an X that looks like a pair of suspenders.

"How come there's only eleven stars?" I ask.

"That's how many states have seceded," Grandpa says. We both look up at the flag. To the North, we might as well be England or China. We are a foreign country now, and I am not sure how I like that.

Grandpa puts his harmonica away and grumbles while he piles his plate with food.

I spot Pa and Henry in the company of men. They are with friends. Henry has lots of friends because everybody likes him. People in Smith County are either Pa's age or Henry's age. Nobody I know is my age. The militiamen show off what all they learned drilling. The captain tells them they're fixing to march away on foot to Enterprise, where they'll board a train to join up with the new Confederate army down at Fort Pickens in Pensacola, Florida. The militia lets out a cheer. Both Pa and Henry get to travel, and I can hardly stand it. The captain dismisses them, saying it's time to meet up with us families and sweethearts and engage in farewell conversations.

When Pa and Henry find us, Pa starts with Buck.

"You listen to my pappy and to Miss Russell now, you hear?" I'm mad that he says Ma and not me. He bends his head close to Buck's as he talks. Some of the other men are taking one Negro with them, but I hear Pa tell Buck he needs him here with me, Ma, Grandma, and Grandpa.

Buck nods and I can't read his face. He stares past Pa, just over Pa's shoulder. Buck doesn't have anybody but us, so he doesn't go off with the rest of the colored folk. Buck never made friends with the other colored people in the county, not because there weren't any his age, or because they did not like him, because most did. No, Buck didn't have friends because he chose not to.

Grandpa stands up and walks over to Pa. He takes off his wedding ring and gives it to Pa. Pa looks at the ring, then at Grandma, who can't see any of this. Grandpa puts his finger to his lips. Pa never wore a wedding ring because, as he says, "Jewry is for womenfolk." Neither Grandpa nor Pa says anything as Pa slips the ring onto his finger.

"Things have gotten too easy for you boys," Grandpa grumbles. "Telegraphs, newspapers, and *rifles* now, not muskets. Everybody's gone soft. This will be a soft, easy war." He sets out to lecture a man who is standing nearby.

"Shanks, you mind your ma, do your reading and writing."

"Yes, sir."

Ma gives Pa the housewife she's made for him, with needles and swatches for mending his uniform. Pa carefully folds the housewife into his haversack, talking quiet and low with Ma. Henry shows me his army rifle, which is about the same size as Henry.

"Grandpa says slavery isn't right or wrong. He says it's just what we're used to," I say to Henry as he shifts his rifle from shoulder to shoulder, showing out.

"Don't you get all girly," Henry says. He sounds different with his uniform on. "We need our slaves and they need us. See those fields?"

Henry and me, we look out at the fields just planted with corn, cotton, and peas. The fields are divided with a few snake rail fences, which roll with the hills all the way to the steep riverbanks. Pa likes to say a man can grow anything in Mississippi. Rice, indigo, cotton, tobacco, peas, corn. The list goes on forever.

"Without slaves, how else do you think we could do all we do?" Henry says.

Buck is a colored boy and he's a slave. I am a white boy and I am not a slave. That's just the way God planned it. I nod at the wisdom of it and of my older brother.

We are still looking when Irene Beall and her ma pass and Henry about drops his rifle.

"Hey, Miss Irene," Henry says.

Irene and her ma greet us. Irene poses like she's in front of an artist ready to paint her, then she says how fine Henry looks in his uniform.

"I plan on doing my part, too," she says. "I'm going to be a nurse."

"You will not," her ma says.

"Will too. I'm the only one in the family who doesn't faint at the sight of blood."

"I will have no daughter of mine fussing over a man's body. Heavens. Now come along."

"That boy's not wearing any shoes," Irene says to her ma. We all look down at my feet.

Irene's ma whispers, "Hush," and tells Irene to mind her manners. Henry just stares at Irene's yellow hair, even after she and her ma have walked away.

Ma calls us to come eat.

"That Irene is ugly," I say, and Henry swats me upside the head with his cap.

Grandma asks what kind of lips Irene has.

"Are they skinny or generous?" she asks. "You can tell a

lot about a person's disposition from her lips. That and eyes. If her eyes are too close together, she's stupid. Same goes for a man. And chins. Does that Irene have a good, strong chin? No chin, no strength."

While we eat, a man by the name of Captain Bill Hardy stands up in a wagon, opens the lapels of his coat, and says, "Boys, I'll take all the bullets that are fired in this war and drink all the blood that is shed, because there won't be any. You will only have to go and make a demonstration of our power and might, and you will all be back home in time to take Christmas dinner with your families."

We all cheer.

After we eat, Ma and Grandma put away the dishes, and Grandma about has a fit when she feels the cup Henry's been drinking out of.

"It's cracked. Henry, I know you know better than to drink from a cracked cup. Don't you ever do that again. Lord only knows how many years you just shaved off yer life."

Ma used to laugh out loud whenever Grandma pestered us about drinking from chipped cups, but now she is extra careful and quiet, packing away the plates and what's left of the food.

There is a horserace, and even though he wins, Mr.

McCollum is disqualified because his horse is part mule. The bass drum taps, and all the soldiers get in line. Soon there are enough tears shed to swim a steamboat.

Pa and Henry line up with the other soldiers. Ma, Buck, Grandpa, Grandma, and me stand, watching the men march away. Even though it is still light out, someone shoots fireworks, never once thinking that they sound too much like gunfire.

"Ma," I say. "Pa forgot to tell me goodbye."

"Hush, Sonny," Grandma says.

Next time I fill Grandma's pipe, I will consider adding gun powder like I done once before.

"Wave," Ma says. "He'll be back soon enough."

And they are gone. Just like that. There is nobody left on the picnic grounds of the Liberty Church, save for the Negroes, the women, a few old people, and all us children.

It is still dark when I hear Grandpa come in. He stayed behind with our mule, Ben, after the picnic, and I forded the river to get us back home while Buck sat in the back of the wagon with Grandma. Grandpa's breath smells of whiskey and his clothes of tobacco as he climbs into bed beside me. We are lucky because we have two beds, and with Pa and

Henry gone there is even more room. Grandma and Ma sleep in the feather bed facing ours. Grandma won't let Grandpa into her bed after he has spent an evening at the saloon. She says dancing and drinking are the devil's work, and besides that, his smell keeps her up.

"You awake, Shanks?"

"Yes, sir."

"Well then, move on over," he says. "Hear that wind kickin' up?"

I hear the trees shaking outside. I scoot over and Grandpa bunches up the corncobs in the mattress to divide the two of us.

"Why'd Mr. Lincoln declare war, Grandpa?"

"'Cause we fired on Fort Sumter. That's right near Charleston, South Carolina, where yer grandma's from. I'd've fired too, if she still lived there."

"Why'd we fire on 'em?"

"Because the Yankees won't let us alone. They think they have a right to tell us how to live."

"They don't think Pa should own Buck, right?"

"That's right."

"But we're good to Buck. Pa give him that patch of land to grow his own vegetables, and Ma makes him a new shirt and a pair of pants every Christmas. Pa says Buck was the best investment he ever made."

"Yer pa gets a lot of work out of Buck. Too much maybe, working him fourteen hours on days there's a full moon. Yer pa wants to get beyond his raising. He's got big ideas for this place. Wants a regular plantation."

"What's wrong with that?"

"Nothin', I suppose. But it's not for me."

Pa never talked about himself. Grandpa says that's because Pa is forward thinking. It's like Pa has always been Pa and he was born with a plow in his hand. Grandpa talks about himself and the past all the time. He can talk Indian with the Indians, and he can hunt for deer using nothing but a bow and arrow. His best friend used to be an Indian leader named Deer Joe, who initiated Grandpa into his tribal family and named him Light Brother. Grandpa saw Deer Joe and his tribe get slaughtered by a Dutch family who wanted their land.

"What *would* Buck do if he was to be free?"

"I don't rightly know. Do a little jig, I suppose. Then get back to work. He'd never survive up north. Climate's too cold for the Negro."

"You think Buck would ever kill us?"

All year there has been talk of the North agitating the colored to murder their white masters in their own beds, but no such thing has happened in Smith County. Not yet.

"I think Buck's got more on his mind than killin'. Now go to sleep."

I can see the outline of Grandpa's face and whiskers in the moonlight, his white hair spread out over the pillow. The walls are bumpy with the wind blowing so hard, and I think about how the rain will sound on the roof, how it will be cold in the night, and how embarrassing it will be to sleep spooning with Grandpa the way Henry and me used to sleep sometimes on cold nights.

Summer 1861

I NEED A NEW LEARNING PARTNER, what with Henry gone.
Ma asks Grandpa and he gives it a try one night after supper.

"What's this?" he asks.

"That's a *E*."

"Oh, Lord. This?"

"*X*."

"I can't put together a word like that."

"It says 'Exodus.' That's the name of this here part we're
fixin' to read."

Grandpa stands up and walks around the room some.

—·—

He is always restless when he spends an afternoon in town and returns to find that nothing has changed since he left. Ma looks up from her sewing. Grandma snores in the bed. Buck is in his shanty, probably eating his supper by now.

"That General Jackson held his ground against the Federals up there in Richmond, Virginia, at that Yankee creek called Bull Run. 'There's Jackson standing like a stone wall.' That's what they shouted. Old Blue Light. That's what his men call him."

I wait for more war news from Grandpa.

"Stonewall Jackson," Grandpa says, looking at Grandma sleeping.

"Are we winning?" I ask.

"What with North Carolina and Tennessee now, I'd say the South's got an outstandin' chance. Might could be. No telling."

Ma sighs, like she's sweeping the air. "Maybe if you just go on and read to your grandpa, Shanks," she says.

So I read to Grandpa about Moses, right up to the burning bush, and I don't mind at all because I like Grandpa, and I'm glad for his company, glad, too, for his agreeing to be my learning partner, because now I can go to him and ask questions about the Yankees and the skirmishes, and he can ask me, too, if he wants, about spelling and such.

Grandpa is finally sitting down. I get to the part when God gives Moses his call, and Moses whines to God that he's just a nobody and he's real doubtful that anybody would listen to him, seeing how he's not too good a preacher because he speaks real slow. I laugh and see if Grandpa thinks it's at all funny, but Grandpa's nodding off, and I look over to Ma, and she puts her sewing down, and together we help him into bed.

Early Fall 1861

BUCK AND I CONTINUE TO FARM PA'S LAND to the best advantage that we know about. Neighbor boys and girls help out. When we need rails for the fences, we have a rail splitting. We have log rollings and fodder pullings. Even the girls come and pull fodder, pick cotton, and hoe in the crops. Sometimes it feels like us children are running the county.

Tid Smith makes a crop of corn, and when the fodder is ripe and ready to pull, Buck and me, we don't hesitate to go and help out. Mrs. Smith is a young Confederate soldier's wife and we call her Tid. I don't know how old Tid is. I can usually guess how old anybody around my age is, but everybody Ma or Pa's age looks the same to me.

We all take two rows apiece. Buck takes the two rows next to my two rows, and Tid takes the two rows on my other side.

Already it's fall and I have grown some since Pa and Henry left. I feel proud with how I outpull the rest of the bunch. I am about even with Buck. When I finish my two rows, I turn back and help Tid get her rows out.

By ten o'clock we all finish and we are hot and tired. There is some nice shade under a pecan tree nearby, and we all sit there and take a rest. The war seems far off, like it's happening in some other world. The boys pull off their hats and begin to fan their faces, and the girls pull off their bonnets and begin to fan and get cool. Buck sits under another shade tree with the other Negroes.

"They'll put slavery back when they realize we can't grow cotton without field hands," Tid says, sighing and fanning herself. "Those Yankees just want to run our lives, is all."

"I hear they got factories up north with folks treated in a filthy way," a boy we call Skeet says. "Nobody looks after those workers like we look after our darkies."

For the first time, I feel a might uncomfortable around that word *darky*. I look over to the other shade tree, where Buck's sitting. He's leaning against the trunk, his long legs crossed at the ankles. Would that word rankle him?

"They are manufacturing people. We are agricultural people." Mary Jane Lugar can be such a Miss Priss.

I have never seen a Yankee, but I listen to Tid and the other children talking about them. Yankees move too quickly, and they got no manners, Tid says. They call buttermilk sour milk and they say it's not even fit for pigs. They talk loud and through their noses.

"How can a body talk through his nose?" Mary Jane wonders out loud.

"They might talk funny, but maybe we should be listening to what they got to say." I whisper this more than say it, so I am taken aback when everybody stops talking about Yankees and stares at me.

"That's stupid, Shanks," Skeet says. "We beat the living tar out of them Yankees at Manassas. They'll listen to us now."

Tid nudges me. "What you got to say to that?"

I shrug. "Just seems like we all gotten so used to this slavery business. I reckon we just pulled Tid's corn. We're field hands now, too, aren't we?"

"They're better suited, honey," Tid says, chewing on a piece of rye grass. We all look over toward Buck and the other

Negroes fanning themselves. "White people can't stand the heat like they can."

"I pulled more than Buck," I say. "And Buck's stronger."

"He's lazy, is all," Skeet says.

"No," Tid says. "I know for a fact that that boy Buck is not lazy. You may be right, Shanks. You children can do this work and so can us women." Tid's got this little smile on her face.

"I didn't mean to say nothin' about womenfolk, Miss Tid," I say.

Tid looks at me square and says, "Shanks, I can throw you."

Everybody, all of us stop our fanning.

What gets me is not what Tid says but how she says it.

"You're not game if you don't do it," I say as quiet as I ever heard myself.

The other girls and boys hear, and Mary Jane yells out, "Tid can throw Shanks!" Then Skeet yells, "Shanks can throw Tid."

Buck looks up, and the Negroes start to gather round, laughing.

Tid looks at me and I look right back at her and all of a sudden we are on our feet. She comes at me and gathers me around the waist, and I grab hold of her around the waist, and there we are, she squeezing me and me squeezing her, and everyone all around us is yelling.

We both squeeze each other harder and this gets to be more interesting than the rassle. Tid is dark-haired and big-bosomed, and up close she smells of ripe peaches. The harder she squeezes, the harder I squeeze back. Soon the crowd gets to hollering, some for Tid and some for me. Buck stands nearby, and I hear him say, quiet like, "Come on now, Mr. Shanks. Do somethin' 'sides squeezin'. Throw her."

It gets to be where somebody has to be the winner. Finally Tid throws me to the ground. She has such a grip on me that I can't get up, but I am laughing and smiling as much as she is. On the ground where we lie, side by side, the sun is on us both and I can feel Tid's soft, warm hip against mine.

"I won," Tid says low and soft and breathless.

We can't even hear what all Skeet and Mary Jane and the other children are saying. A breeze rustles the pulled fodder. I do not feel weak and I do not feel so young anymore. This losing doesn't feel so bad.

I hear bats flying. In the distance we hear a dog bark, then gunfire.

IV

Late Fall 1861

MA WON'T LET ME LEAVE the house again, even though I want to see about the smoke that's blowing up beyond the woods in back of Buck's shack. We stay inside, listening to guns that sound like thunder. Ma works on the loom, talking angry against Pa because he has not written. I tell her that neither Pa nor Henry have written because they do not know how to write, but she says they could both talk out something to someone else, and have that nother person write it all down. At last, the guns stop, and we go to bed. In the morning, Buck and I set out to work in the fields.

Sheriff Matkin comes round, and from where I stand in the corn field, I see Ma come running from the house to meet him, sure that he has some sort of news about Pa or Henry.

Ma is big with child. She told me one night after Pa and Henry left that the stork had come and dropped a baby in her belly, and now it's in there growing like a watermelon on a vine. Her stomach is getting bigger, bigger even than my head. Ma is not a big woman, but she is not birdlike either. Without Pa around, she looks taller.

I quit my hoeing and wave Buck in toward the house for a break.

On the porch, the sheriff tells us that the skirmish was not but ten miles away, and our boys held the Yankees back. There were some casualties—he's not sure of the numbers— and the one schoolhouse that was supposed to open before the war but didn't has become a hospital for wounded soldiers.

"We'll need that cow of yours," he says. Grandpa moans. "And your horse."

"Not the horse," Grandpa says.

The sheriff starts to say something, then looks at us all and stops. We are a sight. Me and Buck are dirty from plowing, our clothes all ragtag. We don't have much cotton left for making cloth. At least the grownups have shoes.

"All right then, keep the horse," the sheriff says. "Long as you all keep your eye out for deserters. Let me know and we'll round 'em up. It's a crime, you know. Desertion."

"Have you heard anything else?" Ma asks.

No, he has not heard anything from either Pa or Henry, but he's come to tell us that our troops are on the move, and some are fortifying Vicksburg, even though that city is strong enough to withstand anything. He looks at Grandpa when he says that the army sure could use more men.

"Well, John, what about it?"

"I told you already, this is not my war. 'Sides that, I was not made to fight."

"You old coward," Grandma sniffs.

"I can fight," I say.

"No," Ma says, making a fuss over me. "Not my baby."

The sheriff just smiles and says they are not accepting ten-year-olds.

"Not yet," Grandpa mumbles.

"Eleven," I say. Everybody but me forgot my birthday last month.

The sheriff asks Ma if we're needing anything.

We still have potatoes, and the apples are just now coming in. We could use more of everything for the coming winter, but Ma is too prideful to ask for flour, coffee, or sugar. She says everything should go to our fighting men.

"Shanks could use more paper," she says.

"I'll look, but rule is if you can't eat it, you don't need it."

"Is there anything we can do?" Ma asks.

"That schoolhouse is getting full up with wounded." He looks at Ma and puts his hat on. "It's too rough a place for you, ma'am, but I know for a fact they need bandages and men. Good afternoon, ladies. Shanks. John." He tips his hat, mounts his horse, and rides off.

"You hear that, Ma?"

"Yes I did. Terrible. Let's see if we can round up some scraps for those bandages."

But I'm not thinking about Vicksburg or bandages. I'm thinking about what all the sheriff said. Maybe if he comes around again, he'll ask me to join up. I'd get a rifle, and Mr. Childre would make me a pair of new shoes like he done for Henry and Pa, and then, then I'd go traveling and see the world.

That afternoon, Buck and me ride to the schoolhouse to deliver bandages and what potatoes and peas we can spare.

Even before we get there, I can smell the burning, and the bad coffee soldiers are boiling up in their oyster cans, and the sweet, oniony smell of vomit. At first, all I hear is the coughing. Then the moaning.

One man leans against the side of the building, chewing on a piece of raw bacon that looks rancid. One of his legs is cut off above the knee, and the bandage around his stump is brown with dried blood. He looks off past me and Buck.

"See the Christmas trees yonder?" he says.

Inside, everything is dirty and everybody smells like sweat and farts and piss and blood, and even as I'm thinking up the words for the smells I'm smelling, I'm thinking of how Ma would wash my mouth out with lye soap just for thinking up such words.

There is blood spattered everywhere. All around us the soldiers use books as pillows, the pages red with blood. There are men with bandages over missing eyes, missing legs, missing hands, and missing arms. There are men with bandages wrapped around so much of them it looks to be that it's just those loose cotton rags, turned brown from the old blood, that are holding them together.

Two soldiers tell Buck and me to step aside while they haul a man up front and lay him across a table that was meant to be the teacher's desk. A doctor with a bloody butcher's apron looks at the man's arm, which is split open down the side, and the blood drains into the pool under the table. Just behind the table is a pile of arms and legs, legs that still have on socks and shoes like they are fixing to walk on out of there by themselves. The doctor picks up a saw.

A soldier who looks to be Henry's age holds out his hand to me.

"Water," he says.

The smell is bad in here, worse than an old outhouse, and I cannot move, but Buck, he just sits himself down beside that poor fellow and wipes his sweaty brow as though he is Henry himself.

I leave them. I pretend like it's all going to be all right.

Outside, it feels safe. There aren't any limbs or dead bodies that I can see. Ma always says cleanliness is next to godliness, that and "Everything has its place in the world." It was bad dirty in that schoolhouse. Surely God wasn't in there.

"They say there were one hundred and twenty-six casualties."

I swing round and see yellow-haired Irene Beall loaded down with rolled bandages.

"And that was only a little tiny piece of fightin'. Somewhere else there's the same going on, but most likely bloodier."

Irene has an old cap on and she looks almost like a boy.

Without all the ruffles and ribbons, she looks better than she looked at the Liberty Church barbecue. I am surprised how glad I am to see her.

"Ma dressed me ugly so I won't attract attention. She doesn't approve of my bein' here, what with so many men, but everybody's got to do her part and I figure if Pa gets hurt, I'd want a me somewhere helping him get better. I understand you brought peas."

We hear shouting and carrying on and we go have ourselves a look-see.

Sheriff Matkin is locking leg irons around the ankles of one of our own men.

"Deserter." Irene spits the word out. "See him, the one with the red hair?"

I nod. The sheriff is attaching what looks to be a fifty-pound ball to his chain.

"He was fighting a battle at Wilson's Creek, in Missouri, standing right beside his best buddy, when a cannonball came and tore off his buddy's head. But I 'spec he's seen worse. This is the third time they caught him for deserting."

I hold my neck and stare at the man, who is shackled now and seated.

"He's a no-good deserter, all right, but imagine that, your

best friend slumping down beside you without a head," Irene says.

"Girls aren't supposed to be talkin' 'bout such things." I felt stomach-sick and wondered why she didn't too.

"I'm just telling you what happened," she says, looking me up and down. "If you're talking and your head gets cut off, your lips still move. You think a head can still have thoughts without its body?"

"What are they going to do with him?" I redirect Irene's attention to the deserter. Just then, Buck comes out of the schoolhouse and stands beside me.

"Well, what they usually do with deserters is whip 'em, shave their heads, strip 'em, and brand 'em with a red-hot iron with the letter *D* on both hips."

"Does your Ma know you talk like this?"

"That man there's already been court-martialed and sentenced to be shot."

"Why don't they just leave him be?"

"They joined up, just like my daddy. Just like your pa and your brother. You can't change your mind."

"Don't seem right to kill our own just for not killing," I say.

"You can be such a child." Irene is smiling a queer smile. "Still no shoes?"

"Come on, Buck, we gotta git."

"My daddy's comin' home real soon," Irene says.

"How's that?"

"The doctor told me they're working on a new rule that says a person who owns twenty Negroes can come home. We got thirty."

The soldier looking out yonder at Christmas trees coughs, then says, "Rich man's war, poor man's fight."

A doctor walks by with a bucket full of arms and legs. He says something and Irene starts off. I suppose she is used to the bad smells and the arms and the legs, and I don't know which is worse—being around this or getting used to it.

"Buck, you all right?" I say, feeling a might stomach-sick. Buck is staring at the red-haired soldier who will be shot for being a deserter.

"Never seen a white man in chains," Buck says.

V

Early Winter 1861

WE ARE IN THE MIDDLE of a drought. Ma worries about what we are going to eat later on in the winter. I worry about what we are going to eat now. Grandma tells me to put aside food for when Pa and Henry come back. I dry as much fruit as we can spare—apples, pears, peach halves—but we keep going through it. Every night before supper, we pray for rain, and before we all go to bed we get down on our knees and ask after that rain again, in case God forgets. Our own soldiers have already come and killed all the hogs we had running wild in the woods behind Buck's cabin. The chickens are long gone, and Buck and I hunt rabbit so Ma can dry the meat in the smokehouse. We plow the land so we can plant us a late crop before hard winter sets in.

Grandpa takes to sleeping under the freak tree in the yard. Two pines crossed one another at one time and Grandpa figures that they grew close together to form an X; then, he says, lightning probably struck, and now the trees look like a Y. He says he feels right sleeping under the trees and that they will probably bring him good luck.

I go out and sit beside him one night, after we eat some crab apple pies Ma made with lard that was just about to turn bad. The eating felt like a feast.

"You still wish you was a soldier boy?" Grandpa asks me.

"I'd make a good one," I say.

"It sure is something," he says. "Everyone wants a place in the picture."

"Excepting you."

"Excepting me."

"We didn't finish up with Moses," I say. It's gotten to be I'm not thinking about lessons or reading anymore, or even what I'm going to say next to Ma to make her smile. I only think about what we can eat and where we can find something to eat.

"You go on, do him yourself."

"What you thinking about?"

"Texas. Land is pure out there. A man can be left alone. Be free."

"Do you think Buck's happy being a slave?"

"Let's not talk about all that anymore now, ya hear?"

We sit looking up at the stars, listening to the cicadas, then a screech owl. The gunfire is way off in the distance tonight. Grandpa points out the Big Dipper, and I pretend like he's teaching me something, even though Henry showed me the constellations long ago, after Pa showed him.

"Buck's different from you and me," Grandpa says after a while. "Now go on in. It's your bedtime."

The following morning, Grandpa packs a clean shirt and a pair of pants into his saddlebag, loads his gun, and saddles up his horse, which is really Pa's horse.

"You old fool," Grandma says. "Our army doesn't need the likes of you."

"I'm not joining up, woman," Grandpa says. "I'm headed west. Maybe I'll join up again with some Indians."

We all, none of us, say a word.

"You're leaving us?" I finally have to ask. "Just like that?"

"Quit looking thataway," he says. "Least I'm telling you."

"You have to tell us because you can't write a note. It's just what you did last time, you mean old fool," Grandma says.

"And I came back, didn't I?"

"Three years later," Grandma says. She gets up without asking anybody for help. She faces Grandpa in the swept yard, her sunken eyes shut. She takes her corncob pipe out of her mouth, then spits. "Shame on you," she says, smoke coming out with the words. She puts the pipe in her mouth and feels her way back into the house.

"Buck, come over here, I got something for you." I can't hear Grandpa as he whispers something to Buck, but I see Buck close his dry, dark fingers around something. He puts it in the right front pocket of his pants.

Ma will not come out of the house to say goodbye to Grandpa. She says she is too busy making cloth out of left-over cotton scraps for the baby, but I know she is too angry for goodbyes.

Grandpa blows out "Swing Low, Sweet Chariot," then gives his harmonica to me.

"You keep this." He reaches into his pocket and pulls out an arrowhead. He gives that to me too. "To make you strong," he says.

I put the arrowhead in my pocket. I don't say nothing, because I don't have words for the nothing I feel.

Ma says everything works out for the good in God's plan, but I'm thinking, how can this be good? And what's the plan? And what kind of experience does God have anyway? Seems like he starts a world, then changes his mind about everybody in it, or regrets the whole idea, the way he did with the flood and all those towns he set out to destroy. When was the last time he came down and said, "Here, let me give you a little hand with that"?

Buck and me, we wave to Grandpa, who turns back and looks when I put the harmonica to my lips and blow. But nothing, not a sound, comes out, and Grandpa just turns right back around and keeps on riding, and it seems like nobody takes no notice.

VI

Christmas Day 1861

AFTER MA AND GRANDMA AND ME eat a potato for Christmas dinner, I tell Ma I don't believe Grandpa has left us for good. She doesn't say anything.

"He'll be back, I just know," I say.

I catch slow-moving fireflies in an old jam jar. Nothing is fun like it used to be, and I only end up feeling bad for the ones stuck in the jar.

I don't miss church. I don't even need presents today. But I am needful of menfolk just now.

Buck is sitting under the freak tree, sharpening the hoes. He wears his Christmas present, the shirt Ma made for Henry last Christmas. In the pocket is Noah's ark, which is really a rough little boat I whittled out of an oak branch and gave to Buck. I am not much of a whittler.

I sit down beside him and watch the road, expecting to see Grandpa or Pa or Henry come riding back home. Way back at the Liberty Church barbecue, Captain Bill Hardy promised everybody that all the soldiers would be home for Christmas. I wonder what other promises have been broken. I pick up a piece of flint and a hoe and start to sharpen alongside Buck. I think about it: Pa is fighting for what he believes, for the South and for slavery. Henry is fighting for what Pa believes. Grandpa doesn't believe in fighting, period, so he up and leaves in the middle of a war, seceding from us and the South both. Who is right?

For a while Buck and I don't say anything. It is enough to sit by him on the saddles of the roots of the tree, cleaning and sharpening our tools for the days of work ahead of us. Buck isn't like other slaves. Nothing surprises Buck. Come to think of it, Buck is not like any colored folk I know of in Smith County. He is neither happy nor sad. He is just Buck. And Buck being just Buck is what I want now.

"I got a Christmas present for you," Buck says. "Come on wid me."

Buck gets up and I follow him to his shack. Pa taught us to respect Buck's privacy even if he was our slave, so I have never been inside Buck's shack. It is neat and clean. The dirt floor is swept, and his mattress, which is stuffed with corncobs, has been shaken smooth. Buck pulls out the only chair, and I set my jar of fireflies on the table and sit down.

"What's that smell?"

"Tea," Buck says. "Want some?"

Buck pours me something warm from a kettle on the table. It smells like tobacco.

"Senna leaves and ginseng root. Helps whatever ails you."

It doesn't taste the way it smells, and it's sweet.

"This is a fine present, Buck. Thank you."

"That ain't your present, Mr. Shanks."

Buck reaches under his mattress and pulls out a soldier's knapsack.

"Wow," I say. "Looks to belong to one of our own. Anything in it?"

I reach in and find a pouch of flat tobacco. I'm not allowed to chew tobacco, because I am in good health and tobacco is only good for children whose health is not very good.

"Found it in the field today," Buck says. "Figured you could make you a pair a dry-weather shoes out of it, there being a drought and all."

I look for holes or tears and don't find a one. I hand Buck the tobacco.

"Thank you, Mr. Shanks."

We drink the tea and look around the room some. We can hear whippoorwills tonight, no gunfire.

"What'd Grandpa give you?" I say.

"Madstone. He say a Choctaw give it to him when he first settled out there in Coffee County, Alabama."

"What else he say about it?"

"S'posed to rid me of my water frights. Carry it on yer right side and yer safe from white masters, too."

I nod. I can barely remember what Pa or Henry or even Grandpa look like. Already their faces are slipping away from me like pieces of shells on the bottom of a bowl of raw egg.

"You ever think about having a family of your own, Buck?"

"No kind of life for a family." Buck shakes his head. "They wouldn't be my own. They'd belong to yer Pa, wouldn't dey now?"

"You'd have someone to keep you company at night."

"I got all the company I need."

The moon is full and it lights the room. I can see Buck's face clearly, the sweat glistening on his forehead. There are no laughlines around his mouth, no crow's-feet from smiling. Nobody really knows how old Buck is. I suppose he's about Henry's age, but he seems much older.

I hear Ma calling for me.

"You want me to set dose bugs loose?"

I forgot about the fireflies.

"I reckon dey die in dere iffen you don't."

We step out onto Buck's porch and I open the jar. They're slow to find their way out, but soon all the fireflies fly away.

"Dere dey all go," Buck says, but I am not watching the fireflies. I am looking at Buck smiling.

VII

Late Winter 1862

MA MAKES BUCK MY NEW LEARNING PARTNER and she commences to teach us both. She says she is sick and tired of living around uneducated men, and where has it gotten her? Where has it gotten the South? She says Buck learning right alongside me will help me.

"Everybody needs a learnin' partner," she says like she has to explain it to me.

He can come into the house now after we've all finished supper and cleaned up, and he can sit at the table right alongside me as long as we both promise not to tell folks. Ma says people get funny when their Negroes know as much if not more than they do.

Buck doesn't make a thing of being too big to sit on the bench, and he looks different inside the house, seated, holding his back straight. He cleans himself up before he comes, and he wears his Christmas shirt.

Right off the bat Buck likes the looks of the alphabet Ma prints neatly on the back page of the Bible. Paper is hard to come by and ink is nearly impossible to get now that the Yankees have closed most all the ports. Ma prints capital letters and what she calls lowercase letters too. Buck has seen letters before, but not all in a row, in proper order and up close like this. He says the *c*'s and *e*'s smile at him, and all those capital letters look like ladders to the sky.

We try our own hand at writing. Buck's print is dark and neat. My ink puddles and smears. Finally Ma reads to us, slow and even, pointing out the letters that make up a word that make up a sentence that make up a paragraph that make up a story. She says she's tired of all the horrors in the Old Testament, and she starts in with the Jesus stories.

Buck and I sit at the table, side by side. If Henry or Pa were here, they'd have called me names, but they are not here. I am. Does it make me less a man because I like being around a colored boy? Maybe they wouldn't mind. I think of the way they were that day I saw them all under the shade tree after working together. Being around someone as long as Pa has been around Buck, and working right alongside him, wasn't that a kind of friendship?

"Those boys will never amount to anything," Grandma says to Ma from her bed. "Why do you bother at all?"

Ever since Grandpa left, Grandma won't get up out of bed. She says she has sick headaches, and she lays there hating. Ma says Grandma has lost hope along with Grandpa and her only son.

"But they're both coming back," I say.

Ma ends her reading. Then we spell out *mother* and *father*, *sister* and *brother*. Ma writes: *My mother loves me.*

"*Me* is the object of that mother's love," Ma says.

"Me?" I say, and Ma laughs and hugs me.

Buck stares down at the sentence.

Ma says, "When you were three, you used to say, 'Ma, I love you sixty much, that's how much I love you.'"

Even though Buck doesn't laugh or even smile during our lessons, I am glad for his company. I wonder sometimes if Buck misses his ma. I wonder if he ever knew his pa. Sometimes I think he is lucky because he doesn't have a ma or a pa, or an older brother who's better at plowing and hoeing and shooting and just about everything, or an old grandma who's gone mean, or a grandpa who up and leaves. Sometimes I think Buck is freer than I am.

In two months' time, Buck learns to write sentences with subjects, verbs, and objects.

Grandma lies in her feather bed for four days and four nights, thrashing and flailing and scratching at her own self, yelling that the niggers are trying to nail her into a pine box, alive. We lift her head and give her water, when she allows us. Every now and then she takes a spoonful of peas.

On the third day, Ma tells Buck to fetch the preacher, Brother Davenport, except when Brother Davenport arrives, Grandma won't see him. He is a tall, big-boned man with thick, heavy hands, dark hair, and deep-set eyes. Brother Davenport says a prayer over her anyhow, and Grandma sits up and spits in his face.

Ma comes rushing over and hands Brother Davenport a cloth. She tells him how Grandma doesn't know her mind now, and he says he understands.

"Do you have any news?" I ask.

He tells us that Fort Donelson, near Shiloh in Tennessee,

just fell to a man named U. S. Grant, and the Yankees say that Grant's initials don't stand for United States but Unconditional Surrender. Brother Davenport leaves Ma with a sack of peas, which she tries to turn down but can't, because he insists.

That night, Ma sits by Grandma's bed, making little socks for the baby, sipping tea she steeps from hazelbrush and blackberry roots. Buck and I sit at the table, and since we don't have any ink left to practice our capital letters, we take turns reading how Jesus stretched two fish and five barley loaves to feed five thousand hungry people with leftovers. Buck and I, our mouths are watering while we read, and all the while I'm thinking how I wish somebody here was Jesus so we wouldn't have to be hungry all the time.

Late that night, Grandma shouts out and Ma lights a candle and tells me to get some water and a cool cloth.

"I bet she wants to tell Grandpa a thing or two," I say, but Ma shushes me quiet.

"We are all sinners," Grandma shouts when I try to put the cool cloth on her forehead. She grabs hold of my arm and squeezes me hard.

"Criminals are we and we'll never be forgiven."

She goes quiet. Too quiet. Her blind eyes look like the dried glaze Ma used to dribble over fruitcakes at Christmastime, back when we had sugar and she baked sweets.

"Ma?"

Ma comes and puts her hand over Grandma's mouth. She bends over Grandma and listens for a heartbeat. Grandma is not blinking, and I know now that she is dead. I feel terrible bad about everything awful I ever done, like that time I put a little gunpowder in Grandma's corncob pipe and it blew up; it didn't hurt her none, just shocked her some. Ma whipped me out by the henhouse while all the chickens ran around going *cluck cluck cluck.*

Ma closes Grandma's eyes and seals them with copper pennies. She straightens herself, her hand on the small of her own back, her belly thrust out. I want to run out of that room, because now Grandma is not Grandma. She is a dead woman, and I don't want to be in the same room as a dead woman, and I don't want to have to bury a dead woman, and it's like Ma knows exactly what I'm thinking because she says, "Go to the schoolhouse and fetch somebody there to help us put Grandma to rest. Take Buck with you. It's not safe to travel at night alone."

We still have our mule, and Buck and I ride him into town.

It's late and dark by the time we get to the schoolhouse, and the moaning the men make sounds like the noise of whispering ghosts. Buck stays outside with Ben.

The man who was looking at Christmas trees is gone now, and I wonder if he's dead, too. I see a man sleeping just where the Christmas tree man had been, except that this man's arm looks alive with movement, and as I get closer I see just what I don't want to see: the white backs of maggots, millions of them, swarming around that soldier's wounded arm. I go on past and leave him. I can only think about now right now.

Irene is not there but Brother Davenport is. He's saying prayers over a moaning soldier. When he looks up at me, I see dark rings under his eyes. The front of his shirt is stiff and brown with old blood. I tell him what I need to tell him, and he says he can't come tonight but will be there sometime tomorrow morning. I thank him.

The night air is cool and smells of rotting apples. We head back and are not but a half a mile into the journey when Buck stops Ben and says, "Listen."

In the quiet I hear the cold sound of iron chains settling. We turn and look. The tall pines stretch monster arms all around us.

"Who's that there ghostin' around these here parts?" I say.

A cloud passes across the sooty sliver of moon, and in the light I catch some of the gray of a uniform from behind a tree trunk. Then he stands before us, his hat on his shoulder, his iron ball on top of his hat. I recognize the red hair.

None of us three has a gun between us, but I can tell Buck to run get Sheriff Matkin.

"Name is Tempy."

"Shanks. This here's Buck."

Buck is staring at Tempy's ball and chain.

"I thought they killed you for desertion way back when, Mr. Tempy," I say.

"I got away. Then I got caught again."

"Oh."

"You boys wouldn't happen to have a saw on you, would you?"

I put my hand in my pocket like I really do have a saw there, but I pull out half a raw sweet potato instead and give that to Mr. Tempy.

He eats it in two bites and tells us how sweet potatoes may have first come from Peru.

"I've had an ear of corn in the last five days. That and any rat I can find," he says. "I thank you."

"Where you goin'?"

"Julius Caesar crossed the Rubicon to start a civil war, only to come home and be murdered by conspirators. I'm gonna get as far away as I can get."

"Where you from?"

"Missouri. Border state."

We hear dogs barking in the distance, back near town.

"They set the hounds after you," I say. "You best take to the water. The Leaf River ain't but a few yards thataway."

I point toward the dark woods behind Tempy.

"We live about a quarter of a mile east. There's an ax by the woodpile near the house. You can use it if you want."

Buck is looking at me. The words come out of me solid and sure.

"I'm grateful to you, Shanks."

"You'd best rub the soles of yo' shoes wid dese here wild onions," Buck says and hands over a fistful of onion greens. "Keep dose dogs away."

Tempy nods and is gone before I can say anything more. Buck and I, we both of us climb up on the mule and steady ourselves for the ride back. We start up again, faster this time because I don't want to face any dogs or the sheriff.

"That ball must weigh fifty pound," Buck says.

"It'll take a while. If they don't catch him, that is."

"That Sheriff Matkin sure must not have trusted Mr. Tempy," Buck says after a spell.

Buck says you can tell how trustworthy a slave is by the size of his irons. When a master buys a slave, he puts an iron band first around his leg, then later around his arm; when a smaller band is finally placed around his finger, it means the slave is the master's almost trusted one.

"'Cept Pa never put no band around you," I say.

"That's right," Buck says. "Only one wearing a band is your pa, and that's his pappy's old wedding ring."

"How d'you know about those onions, anyway?"

"Heard tell," Buck says. "Hear pepper works, too."

Ma is on the corncob mattress, moaning and yelling, while Grandma still lies in the feather bed with the pennies over her eyes.

"The baby's coming, Shanks. Have you got a doctor or the sheriff with you?"

I look at what I got with me and I am thinking, I cannot believe that Grandpa just up and left us. Already Buck is at the stove, fixing to boil water.

"We need more wood for the stove," Ma says.

I go outside and hear a *clank clank clank* at the woodpile. There is Tempy, an escaped deserter sentenced to die, holding up his freed arm.

"You know anything about birthing babies?" I ask.

"Ma, somebody come." I am standing in the doorway with an armload of cordwood.

Tempy's looking none too fine. His clothes have dried out from the river water, but his red hair is hanging down loose and greasy, dark circles ring his eyes, and he's got an old rag tied over the black cuff that is still clamped around his wrist.

"A soldier?" Ma says, breathless.

"Midwifery is a skill dating back to the fifteenth century," Tempy says. "It's somethin' I know somethin' about, more than soldiering. Shanks, Buck, you two wait outside unless I call for your assistance."

He is already at the pot of water, washing his hands. I keep thinking that Grandpa, Pa, and Henry are all going to come marching in any minute.

"That other lady in the bed don't look too well," Tempy says.

"That's Grandma and she's dead." I didn't expect to shout so.

"I'll call if I need your help," Tempy says, his voice real strong and calm. He is putting Ma's pillows on the floor, helping her to sit up even though she wants to stay down.

"The Choctaw taught me this, Ma'am. It's the best way."

"We got an escaped convict in there teaching Ma to give birth like an Indian," I tell Buck on the porch. "Pa's gonna have my hide."

Buck just laughs and tells me Tempy looks like he knows what he's doing. "More din us," he says. "'Sides that, yer Pa ain't here, is he now?"

"You think Grandma being in there dead and all is bad luck?"

Buck looks out toward the tree shaped like a Y. "Can't say that I knows fer sure."

I hear Ma moaning.

"What you figure a rat tastes like?"

Buck doesn't figure long. "Like snake."

After a long spell, we hear the catlike mewing of a new baby crying. Tempy comes out, bare-chested and smiling.

"Congratulations," he says. "You have a new baby sister just as dark-haired and mysterious as a young Cleopatra."

"And Ma? Did you hurt Ma?"

"Your Ma is just fine. Worn out, but fine."

Sure enough, Ma is inside, sitting up in bed, holding the tiny pink baby, who is wrapped in Tempy's shirt.

"Come meet your itty-bitty baby sister," Ma says when she sees me.

"She's just a bit of a thing, idn't she?" I say, staring down at her half-closed eyes, her wrinkled little hands that are more like paws. She has dark hair, just like Tempy said.

"Bit," Ma says smiling. "Let's call her that. Bit."

I smile, proud that I come up with a name.

"Hey, little Bit," I say.

"I'll need some chamomile and rose hip from the garden," Tempy says. "Your mama's going to need a nice hot pot of tea."

"In a little bit," I say, and when we all laugh I think how long it's been since we done that.

We eat the morning's corn bread, and we roast chinquapins, which taste like chestnuts. Tempy keeps Ma with a steady supply of tea. He doesn't have a gold coin, so he puts a chunk of quartz in the palm of Bit's hand so that she will have financial success in later life. After a while, both Ma and the baby fall asleep, and we three sit out on the porch.

"Oh, I wish I was in the land of cotton." Tempy sings real slow and quietlike. He can barely carry a tune in a bucket. "Old times they are not forgotten."

"What was the worst you seen?" I say.

"Look away, look away." Tempy takes as deep a sigh as I ever heard.

"I suppose you boys want to hear about shootin' and bangin' away up yonder. You don't need to be thinking about our men dirty and vomiting blood and half torn apart and dying."

"How come you don't want to fight no more?" Buck says, point blank.

Tempy stares at Buck. Buck hardly ever looks anybody in the eye, let alone a white man, but he does now. Tempy says he will tell us, seeing how we have a right to know.

"I'm the tiredest man you want to know." He laughs and tilts his chair on its back legs. "Tearing up towns and railroad tracks and bridges is all I been doing for the last year. Tearing up things and killing. That's the war. And for what? So people can go on keeping slaves and growing what they grow down here. It just shouldn't be so."

He allows his chair to thump down on all four legs.

"Now mind you, I don't hate the South. I just hate slavery

and I hate the war, but most of all I hate slavery. It's even worse than war."

"Are you a Yankee spy?" I ask.

"No, son. I'm not. I'm terrible with maps, too."

After a spell, I ask if he ever met up with Pa or Henry. Tempy shakes his little head and says he didn't see or know either one of them.

"Most likely dead by now," he says.

What he says hits me. It is a thought that has never come across my mind until the minute he said it.

"Those Yanks aren't going to be satisfied until ever last one of us is dead. They're breeding up north, you know. Just so they can come down here and destroy everything that is of the South."

Tempy sounds like Brother Davenport, but he's not saying Brother Davenport things. He doesn't say we must trust in our kind, Heavenly Father. Tempy never says anything about God.

"No," he goes on. "This war can't be finished 'til everybody's killed."

We hear dogs barking in the distance. Tempy stands and tells us how he is much obliged for the good supper. He was awful hungry. Buck and I stand up, too.

Tempy takes one long last drink of well water, then he

looks to where Buck is standing. The two of them are about the same height and build.

"You comin'?" Tempy asks.

We stand there for what seems like a long time, but I know it is only minutes. I hold my breath, thinking how at the beginning of the evening I thought I was going to lose Ma, when all along I was really going to be losing Buck.

Most all the Negroes all around us are leaving in the night, probably rubbing pepper or onion grass on the soles of their shoes to keep the hounds off their track.

Buck can go with Tempy. He and I both know I will not stop him. But I don't want Buck to go. I am not thinking about Buck, I am only thinking about me.

Buck looks at me, then at Tempy. The barking dogs don't sound closer but farther off. They must have gone another way.

"Wait right heah," Buck says. He leaves the house and goes back to his shack, where I imagine he gathers together what he has—his Christmas shirt, which has become his studying shirt, the oak ark I whittled for him, the madstone Grandpa left him, which was supposed to cure his water fears. What else does he have?

Buck comes back holding his Christmas shirt and the

pouch of tobacco I gave him, the one that was in that canvas bag he found while plowing a field that day.

Buck gives Tempy the shirt, then the pouch. "Good for chewing. I'll be staying here, but thank you, Mr. Tempy, sir."

Tempy puts the shirt on and takes the tobacco. "You're not a thing but a dog here," he says. "You can leave."

"I knows that, sir," Buck says. "But I'm not thataway."

I never saw Buck shake anybody's hand before, but like most things, Buck knows how just as good as I do. I can't hear what all they say to one another, but Tempy laughs and puts his hand on Buck's shoulder. Outside on the porch, we hear hounds in the distance, like now they figured out their way.

"You better git," I say. I want Tempy to leave now, before Buck changes his mind.

"I 'spec you'll stay too, won't ya son?"

"I'm not leaving, if that's what you mean."

"A man of the South," he says, putting his hand on my head like I'm a child. "You will forever live under the shadow of ruins, my boy." He says this like he's Brother Davenport saying a blessing.

When Tempy finally leaves, Buck and I sit down on the steps.

I wonder out loud if we have done something terrible

wrong by not alerting officials about Tempy. Buck shakes his head and says he doesn't expect so. He says Mr. Tempy is a man worn out with killing and he should be set loose now.

If they are still alive, Pa and Henry must be worn out, too. Worn out with the cold and the rain and sleeping on the ground. Worn out with the hunger and the dying and the killing and all that blood.

We can hear the dogs again, and the screech owls.

I think on what Buck said about leg irons and bands, but Buck doesn't have any ball and chain that I can see or think of. And it occurs to me right then that these slave rules aren't God's rules, they're *our* rules.

"How come you didn't run off?" I ask Buck. "Most all of them down at the Beall plantation ran off."

"I figured I been around you all all my life," he says and just leaves it at that.

It's dark out and I know he can't see me. Still I want to thank him, but my throat chokes up and I can hardly swallow, so I bump his arm with my elbow.

"You like to fall over and die when you seen yer mama fixing to give birth," he says.

"Shoot," I say. "White as a ghost, you was."

Buck stretches. He is as long and lean as a railroad track.

"Me living in the shadow of ruins. What you think ol' Tempy meant by that, Buck?"

"Can't say that I know any man's mind. May mean you be eatin' rat meat soon 'nough." Buck stands up. "Night, Mr. Shanks." He steps down off the porch and heads for his shack. I stare at his back and his broad shoulders.

"Good night, Buck."

Brother Davenport comes to help Buck and me bury Grandma out behind the house, south of the cutting garden. Grandma is the first Russell to die in Mississippi, and she is the start of our family burying ground. Buck puts together a pine box, and I leave the two pennies on her eyes before we close her up. I don't know why Ma put the pennies over Grandma's eyes, and I don't ask. Maybe it's just to keep her eyes shut. A rock would do just as well, but I imagine a rock isn't dignified the way a copper penny is. Maybe Ma put the pennies there to keep the maggots from getting into Grandma's sockets, or to keep her spirit from jumping out through her eyeholes. Or maybe Grandma just needs the money to get through Saint Peter's gates.

Brother Davenport tells us that the Confederates still have Vicksburg and that we should all feel lucky, lucky to be alive, luckier still because a dangerous man was out by our wood-pile, using our ax to cut himself loose from his ball and chain.

When we are alone, I tell Ma about how Buck had the chance to leave but didn't. She gives Buck Grandma's old Bible which he can keep for his own. Buck covers the Bible with a piece of deerskin.

I never ask Buck anymore about his leaving. I know that either he won't leave or he can't, and I really don't want to know why. I am only glad that he stays, grateful that me and Ma and little Bit have him with us.

VIII

Spring 1862

I FEEL BAD FOR NOT FEELING WORSE about Grandma. Fact is, Grandma's dying just makes me feel old, and feeling old puts sparking in my mind.

Irene Beall lives not but five miles away on a big plantation where the land is level and flat, not far from where the Leaf River forks into the Tallahala Creek. I am almost twelve years old, and I am ready to see Irene, but I have no shoes and I have no experience sparking.

I am not able to dress up very fine. Ma makes all our wearing apparel at home on the spinning wheel Pa built from a poplar sapling. Ma finally got hold of one needle with which to sew, but there is no indigo for dying fabric, and there is no cotton left for spinning. We are even out of patches for the holes in the clothes we wear now.

The way to make shoes in the usual way is to first get some hide from a cow or an ox, stretch it on the back of a barn, and let it dry for a certain length of time. Then take the hide down to the creek, throw it into the water, and let that hide stay there until it's soaked through and through. While the hide soaks, go to the woods and cut down a hickory tree. Saw it up and bring it to the house to burn until it is ashes. Then get the hide and lay it out flat and stretched, and pour ashes all over the hair. Let the ashes stay on the hair until the hair slips off. That's called hairing the hide.

Then you set the hide in a trough in layers of red oak bark, then stretch it over an oak beam and cure it with a curing knife, scraping it good and clean. *Now* the leather is ready to use.

I don't need to do any of this with the soldier's knapsack Buck give me. We haven't had rain in a good long while, so I set out to make me a pair of dry-weather shoes.

Yesterday Buck and I finished plowing the field. Tonight, after cleaning up our supper of dried apples and sweet potatoes, I find the scissors Pa used for making shoes. They are in a box under the big feather bed Grandma died in. The box also contains a pattern for a shoe, a large sewing needle, some thread Ma has spun out of cotton, a few extra pieces of leather for the soles, and some small wooden pegs Pa cut from a hickory tree when he last made a pair of shoes. Sitting there on the bed with Pa's shoebox, using Pa's pattern, and cutting the knapsack the way I seen Pa cut, I can almost see Pa there with me in the room, telling me how to go about making my first pair of shoes.

It takes me three nights. They both look alike, and it does not make any difference what foot either shoe is worn on. If they were leather, they would be tough to break in, but these are my dry-weather shoes—all cloth except for the tip on the toe and a leather spur heel and sole.

I wear them during my lesson. I cannot understand why Ma and Buck smile so much. Finally I put down the story we are reading, about how Judas came and kissed Jesus and finked on him, and I say, "What in tarnation is so funny?"

Little Bit makes a gurgly noise, and Ma asks me, don't I think my shoes will be awful hard to walk in, them being as big as they are? I tell her I used Pa's pattern, and then both she and Buck laugh, and Ma's eyes get all watery.

"Now what is it?" I ask.

"I guess the Lord really did mean for you to follow in your Pa's footsteps," she says, laughing and crying and kissing the top of my head all at once.

"Turn me loose," I say, still sore about them laughing at me. "It's too hot for kissing."

Like I say, I've never been sparking before, and next morning as I get dressed and put on my new shoes and flop out of the house and head for Irene's plantation, I am excited and even a little scared. I take the arrowhead Grandpa left me and I put it in my pocket. "To make you strong," he said. Ma won't let me take Buck for company. She says life and work still have to continue, sparking or no sparking.

On down the road, I have some difficulty walking but I set my mind on how I will manage the approach. I will say, "Evenin'," and she will, too. If things progress too quickly and her ma asks me if I come for any good, I will answer, "Yes, ma'am, but I do not have my business arranged to make any definite moves at present."

I practice my "Evenin's" as I walk. They all come out too fast, so I slow them down some to sound more casual-like.

A man on horseback stops me on the wayside and asks me if I am going to visit a girl. I say, "Yes, sir. I'm going to see

Irene." I wonder what this man sees that makes him know that I am going sparking.

Before I get to the big house, I pass a slave boy hoeing the kitchen garden. He looks to be about my age, and I wonder why he hasn't run off with the rest of them.

"What you smiling at?" I say, and he nearly jumps. He looks down at the ground fast. Pa tells me the Negroes who act this way are usually the ones whipped on a regular basis.

When I get to the big house, I hail at the gate. Irene's house is the biggest one around, but it needs whitewashing.

A colored woman leads me in to where a group of women are standing in a circle, holding the edges of a quilt they have just finished. Irene is holding one of the corners. One of the ladies throws a white cat in the middle of the quilt, and they all laugh as they watch the cat try to make its way out. Finally the cat leaps up and out toward Irene, scratching her knuckles before leaping to the floor.

"Irene will be the first to get married!" a woman screeches.

Irene holds her fingers to her mouth and just that minute sees me. She is wearing an orange dress. She has big blue-green eyes and the kind of yellow hair Grandpa would play into a song.

"What you lookin' at?" she says.

"Irene!" her ma says. "Shame on you. Come on in here, Shanks."

"Such a shame there are no men left," Mrs. Thompson says. Irene's ma tends to Irene's hand while the other ladies fold the quilt. No one else takes any notice of me. I wait, listening to their slow talk.

"What in the world would Mr. Lincoln do with all those slaves if he freed them?"

"I heard he's going to send them to Central America."

"Did you see his picture in the paper? Ugliest man I ever laid eyes on, with those big ears and dark, evil snake eyes."

"He's the devil."

"Who's winning, does anybody know?"

"Depends on who you talk to."

"So many died at Shiloh."

"And now they've got New Orleans and closed all the ports."

"But our Stonewall Jackson defeated the Federals at Front Royal in Virginia. That's in the Shenandoah Valley. That's what my Louis wrote me."

"My Joseph says he's worn out marching."

"Those Yankees are so cold and mean, marching back and forth, stealing all our hogs and yams."

"Well, we still have Vicksburg and we still have the river," Irene's ma says.

I step aside as, one by one, the lady quilters leave, still laughing and talking, carrying their baskets of colored calico and thread. A few of the older ladies greet me and ask after Ma and the baby. I tell them we are holding up well enough.

Irene's ma sends Irene and me out to the porch, where we set down and look out toward a chinaberry tree.

"We are descended from Huguenots," Irene says. "That makes us aristocratic. Those Yankees are all just a bunch of witch burners, come over in the *Mayflower*."

We talk for a while about the drought and how her Huguenot pa is surviving on the same rat meat Tempy ate— that and horseflesh and "coffee" made from roasted peanuts.

"I thought your pa was coming home," I say.

"Any day now," Irene says.

She pulls out a letter she's gotten from her pa and reads it out loud. He wrote how he had to sleep on the ground, how cold it was getting up there in the North, but not to despair, "the Lord is on our side." She folds the letter back up and puts it back in her pocket. I say how nice it must be to get letters.

I don't want to talk about the war anymore. It doesn't

make anything here easier or better and it only makes everybody think about the older, stronger men who aren't with us, when in fact it is me, Shanks Russell, who is sitting right here next to Irene on her front porch.

"You see my shoes?"

"Yes, I did note them."

Off in the distance a Negro boy comes in from his day's work, and we listen to him singing that song about the Promised Land.

"That's little Martin," Irene says, waving at him. "He was born here." Smiling now, Martin waves back.

Irene's mother comes out to the porch with some cool tea. She apologizes that the tea is not sweet, it being impossible to get sugar. But the tea does taste sweet, and I figure Irene's ma has found some sugar to slip in just for me, and this makes me feel she's on my side. Irene's ma talks nice to me, saying how good it is to have a young man as company for a change, it being so sad around the house what with the drought and the war and Irene all melancholy with her pa away. She says she made Irene quit her nursing and helping out at the schoolhouse because her ma says it was making her too rough.

"You'll stay for supper?"

"Yes, ma'am. I'd sure like that."

In the Bealls' kitchen house, some little distance from the big house, they have a long table laden with a good supper, and Irene's ma asks me to be seated at the head of the table. There are seven in Irene's family, three great big boys all younger than me, two baby girl twins, Irene, and her ma. They don't look to be suffering from lack of food—not like everyone else. There is venison and plenty of bread. Irene's ma sees me looking at the bread and says she just got corn from town that day, that because of the scarcity of corn the board of county supervisors bought 6,000 bushels of corn out of Cairo, Illinois, and paid $1,060 for it. I nod in awe at such a sum of money.

Little Martin comes in with a big loaf of bread. Irene's ma tells him to bring it over. He puts it down in front of me, backs away, and stands off to the side. While I break the bread, I can't understand why Irene's brothers are laughing so heartily.

"You boys ought to be ashamed of yourselves," Irene's ma says. "Stop your laughing."

This only makes the matter worse.

I proceed to break up the bread and pass it, and things get quiet as we all partake of the supper.

After supper, we vacate the kitchen house and proceed to the big house. The brothers run off, and with them goes all the pep out of my sparking expedition. I just sit on that porch with Irene, fingering the arrowhead in my pocket, but it's no good. I've got nothing else to do or say.

Just then it starts to rain. It comes down hard, and we can hear all the whooping and hollering from Irene's brothers. It is five miles home for me, and now it is dark and raining.

"Stay the night." Irene's ma stands in the doorway holding a lantern. She puts a pallet out for me in the twin's nursery, and I am glad for this because I couldn't stand to hear any of those boys laughing at me anymore.

As I lie on that pallet, listening to the sound of the rain on Irene Beall's roof, I think how I should be glad to be spending the night in such a big, fine house. After all, I am lying under the same roof as Irene. But all I feel is stupid.

Next morning, I don't wait for breakfast, even though I wonder if it will be eggs and more of that good bread. I thank Irene's ma and go out to the lot and head home. Before I get too far aways, I see Martin sitting out on his porch. It's Sunday and he looks happy not to have to work. For a minute I wish I am him.

When I return home, Ma asks me how my introductions went and I say fine. I set out to find Buck.

My stay at Irene's is my first night away from home, and everywhere I look, I see broken things that need fixing, fields that need weeding, and nuts that need gathering. I can't look at trees and think about climbing them anymore. I am looking at trees to find food.

I tell Buck all I can about the evening at Irene's, then I ask him what he reckoned those big boys up at the big house were laughing at me for.

He shakes his head and looks at my feet.

"Dey laughing at yo' shoes, Mr. Shanks."

I look to see what he is seeing. The way home was wet and muddy, and now my shoes are wet and muddy, too. You can see the outline of my feet through the soggy canvas, and since my feet are about half the size of the shoes, the tips hang limp and my shoes look like a joker's shoes I once seen on one of Grandpa's playing cards, except I don't feel like a joker and I'm not laughing.

I sit under the freak tree every night from here on out, and sometimes I get up to see about things and look down the road.

Summer 1862

IN JUNE WE RUN OUT OF SALT, and we can't afford to buy any more corn. Brother Davenport comes by so that we may "dedicate" our mule Ben to the army services. Now the only farm teams we have are ourselves.

We hear about how Union troops came tearing into Tid Smith's place, took her last pig, and slaughtered it on the grand piano. They hung the meat on their belts and went riding off on their horses, leaving Tid with the pig's head draining blood on her ivory keys.

Union soldiers have just gone through the western side

of the county, and everybody that has anything buries it to keep the Yankees from finding it. Ma says we don't have much worth burying.

In the third week of June, Ma gets word that the Beall twins have scarlet fever. Even though Ma knows I don't want to go back over there, she sends me over with three potatoes. She tells me to leave them outside someplace where they can find them but not to go inside the house, so I won't catch the fever.

Irene sits on the porch, sunburned and thin. Her yellow hair hides inside her dirty bonnet, and she has dirt under her fingernails from working in the fields.

I sit beside her on her porch as we done before, except I feel like she and I are two old people now. I have grown up a good bit, and I am wearing Pa's old work clothes and boots, but Irene takes no notice.

"Pa's dead." She says this in a tired, hopeless way, cradling the three potatoes and staring out at the stump that used to be a chinaberry tree. "And right now the only thing I have on my mind is eating and sleeping."

X

Fall 1862

WE DO NOT EAT, because there is not much left to eat. Buck reads to Bit about Jonah and the whale while Ma tries to mend my britches with the last needle she has. I am learning the multiplication table to keep my mind off food.

Buck sees him first when he looks out the window. He yells for me and Ma to come see quick.

Carrying two withered little peach trees under one arm, Pa comes down the road from the east, walking with a mighty limp.

I go tearing out after him.

I am crying because I am so happy, and I don't remember the last time I was happy, it seems so far back. Maybe when Bit was born. I don't know when I ever cried for being happy. You cry when you're sad, but I'm crying now because I'm happy and relieved all at once. Even though the world's gone topsy-turvy, today I'm all right with it.

First thing Pa does is drop the peach trees and hug me and hold on to me good and tight with one hand, and all at once I understand that he only has one hand, one arm. His left arm is gone and I don't say anything and neither does he. He's dirty and he smells bad, and all I feel are his bones. He gives me his rifle, almost throwing it at me like he don't want it anymore. His eyes, they look, well, they look poor. He picks up the peach trees and we walk the rest of the way back to the house.

Buck is holding Bit.

"Who's this?" Pa says.

"That's Buck, Pa."

"I know Buck," Pa says. "Buck, you have you a new baby?"

"Not mine, Mr. Jack, sir. Yours."

Pa goes white. He looks into the bundle in Buck's arms. There are tears in his eyes now.

Ma comes out of the house crying. She has on the hoop

skirt she wore to the barbecue that day we said goodbye to the soldiers. She doesn't say anything about Pa's arm either, and I'm relieved.

"Oh, my love," I hear her whisper into Pa's ear, and I don't turn away, either. Seems like it has been a century since I last heard that word *love*.

"Henry?" Ma says.

"Yeah, Pa," I say, looking past him and up the road. "Where's Henry?"

Pa shakes his head, and he and Ma, they hug each other. Bit gurgles and Buck rocks her. It makes me feel like nothing, getting the news that Henry is dead.

We go into the house and Ma gets a chair for Pa to sit in. She bustles around trying to find some food to put out. Pa is skin and bones, and his hair and whiskers are as white as ginned cotton.

"I'm not here on furlough, Ma," Pa says. "Ball went through my leg. Lost three toes to frostbite. And then there's just the one arm. I'm no good to the army no more, praise be."

We have us a coming home feast without the feast. Ma brings out the soup she made of potato peels and a hog bone that was left over from something else. Ma can make anything out of nothing now—soups, clothes, babies. Still, we don't have any corn left for bread.

Ma tells Pa about Grandma and Grandpa, and Pa doesn't say a word, just lifts his spoon to his mouth over and over. I wonder if he even hears us, or if he is still hearing the bullets whizzing past. His face is blank and tired. Pa has the same look now as Buck always used to.

It's like I'm seeing through Pa's eyes, and for the first time I notice we are eating and drinking from cups and plates that are all cracked and broken, and we don't care at all. I wonder if this is the cause of Henry's dying, or if we're cutting years from our own lives.

After we eat, I follow Pa outside to the porch. I start playing on Grandpa's old harmonica. I've gotten good and I want him to hear.

"Quit that, will you?" he says and looks up at the sky. I put the harmonica back in my pocket.

"Seems like Buck's become a regular part of the family." He lights a pipe. Pa never smoked before he went off to war. "And it looks like Ma cooked the last mouthful."

I am twelve years old now, nearing the age Henry was when he went off to war. Standing next to Pa, I see I am grown as big as Pa, seeing how he's shrunk a little. I wish I could take back those times I wanted to poke Henry in the eye or wish he was dead. I feel bad for ever thinking such things, and I hope my thoughts didn't have anything to do with his dying. I feel bad that I am even here, on the porch with Pa, and Henry is not.

I look out at what Pa sees, thinking there isn't much to see. The fences are torn down. I tell him the cow, the mule, and the oxen were taken away by our own Confederate troops about the time Grandpa left. The three hogs we left to scavenge for acorns in the woods are long gone, too. Buck and I planted what seed we could get our hands on—corn, cotton, peas. The corn and peas are for us to eat. The cotton is for Ma to weave our clothes out of. Already the weeds are getting thick again.

What we have is barely enough to live on, and we've run through most of it. We have no provisions. We have nothing left to sell. Pa left us with plenty of money, but it is Confederate money, and Confederate money is dead.

"Ma keeps saying how we're the lucky ones," I say, shaking my head after I tell Pa the tally.

"Yer ma is right," Pa says. "We are here. We are still here."

First Manassas, Second Manassas, Pea Ridge, Shiloh,

Antietam. I have heard about the big battles and about the smaller skirmishes and what Grandpa liked to call the "skedaddles." I wonder if Pa ate rats, mule, or dog. I wonder about the land, the Yankees, and the misery he saw. I wonder how many men he killed. I know it must have been terrible to see, but I still wish I'd seen it.

"How did Henry die, Pa?"

Pa shakes his head and turns away. I can't see any part of his face. With his back turned, he looks like a vulture. "You know our situation better than I do, Shanks. What are we going to do?"

I have never in my life heard Pa talk like that, not to me anyway. And even though we are bad off, and I feel tired and too old for twelve, I like that he says what he says, wanting to know what I think. It is the first time he has ever asked me what to do.

I tell Pa about Brother Davenport, who I say is a hard-shelled preacher but a good man, and who has a lot of corn and meat he raised on his farm, and when the Yankees came through he took the stuff down to his church brother's house, thinking this church brother was a poor man and the Yankees wouldn't hunt for anything from him.

"The Yankees didn't hunt from us and they didn't hunt

from that poor man, so Brother Davenport gave some of the food to the poor man and took the rest back for himself."

Pa nods and says he knows Brother Davenport.

"I know for a fact that he has some corn and meat stored away," I say.

Pa steps down off the porch, and using the bayonet on his rifle as a shovel, he starts digging a hole that I don't ask about. I know Pa is tired, but by the way he digs I also know he would never let me give him a proper shovel, nor would he let me dig even if I were to ask.

Pa stops digging, walks about eight feet, and commences to digging another hole. When the second hole is about two feet deep, same as the first, Pa goes inside the house and comes back with those two withered peach trees. He plants the trees. Then he tells Buck to go get some water for them from the well. Pa stands back and watches Buck fetch the well water and water the trees.

"Sure wish Pappy was here to see us now," Pa says. "Everything and everybody in such a poor state. Nothing much civilized about this. He always did like a challenge. Make a man out of you, he'd say."

What I really think Pa means is he is glad Grandpa left us

when he did. Not happy-glad but relieved-glad that his pa doesn't have to see us like we are now.

"Shanks," Pa says. "We'll go up to Brother Davenport's home and see if he'll let us have a little corn."

"When?"

"Soon."

Pa's old clothes hang on him. He hitches his britches up with a rope belt, then sets out and wages war on the weeds in the corn field.

XI

Winter 1862–63

WE EAT EVERY LAST CRUMB in the house before Pa finally makes up his mind to go to see Brother Davenport. Buck and I set out to borrow a wagon and oxen from Mr. MacLaurin, our neighbor five miles out. We take the wagon and oxen and drive back to our house to pick up Pa. He has his rifle. I don't say anything about it, figuring that it has become a kind of habit for him to bring it along, like smoking now, or putting on a hat.

When we get to Brother Davenport's home, Pa and I leave Buck to mind the oxen.

We hail at the gate and Mrs. Davenport tells Pa that her husband is down in the field, planting potatoes.

Brother Davenport is nothing like when I last saw him. He no longer looks like a man who sits and reads and writes and thinks and talks all day. When I shake his hand, I can feel the hard, rough calluses.

In the field, Pa is the spokesman altogether. First the morning greeting is exchanged. Then they talk some about the war and their general devastations. Only then does Pa say, "Parson, we have come to see if we can get a little corn from you."

Brother Davenport stops planting and looks down at the ground for a moment or two.

"Mr. Russell, I don't know that I have got any corn to spare."

Pa looks down at the ground like he's dropped something.

"Parson, we didn't know whether you could let us have any or not. I've put up my time in the war and I come home and found my family entirely destitute without anything to live on, and we have come to see if you would let us have a little corn."

Brother Davenport quits his planting altogether and looks at Pa. "Well, let's us go to the house."

Mrs. Davenport has already fixed a plate for Buck, who is eating in the wagon. Brother Davenport draws a bucket of cool water from the well. We take a drink of water, and the preacher tells us to have a seat in the gallery. He excuses himself and goes into the kitchen, where his wife is preparing dinner. We hear some chickens squalling around in the yard. We don't see any more of the preacher until he comes out and announces that dinner is ready.

Pa and me, we bathe our faces and hands and we go through the house to the dining room. We pass by a piece of furniture called a slab. Though Brother Davenport is a preacher, on this piece of furniture there is a decanter of whiskey, and he asks us if we would have a toddy. It is my first sip of whiskey, and it feels like fire going down my throat. It is awful stuff.

After we partake of the preacher's good dinner, we all sit down in the gallery.

"Mr. Russell, how much corn did you want?" Brother Davenport asks.

"Parson, it is not what we want. It is what can we get."

Brother Davenport puts his hands on his legs and rises to his feet. "Have your boy drive the wagon around to the crib."

By the time Buck and I get to the crib, Brother Davenport

is standing in the crib door. He looks into the wagon, and when he sees Pa's rifle he stops what he's doing.

"Mr. Russell, what about that gun?"

Pa looks down, then up at the sky. I can see that Pa does not know what to say about the gun. Was he really going to use it?

"Parson." He swallows, then looks down at the ground. "We come after some corn."

It could be the whiskey toddy or it could be the big noontime meal and the hot day, but Brother Davenport and Pa both cry then. I have never seen any such thing. I look to Buck, and he just stares straight ahead at the road.

We are losing the war. I can feel it. The South is losing, and surely Mississippi is losing the most. Pa has lost his arm and some toes and, most of all, his firstborn. Has that made him weak? I look to Pa again and feel the stinging in my eyes, and even though I try to stop myself, I cry; and as I recall how Henry used to tell me strong men don't ever cry, I cry even more.

We cry and cry, not like babies but like grown men. Even as I'm crying, I can feel the difference. I am not hurt, but my insides ache and my shoulders shake. I am so ashamed of Pa.

I hear Pa barely whisper, "My boy, my boy," and Brother

Davenport throws his arm around Pa's trembling back. Pa covers his face with his one hand, and the ring Grandpa gave him catches the sun's light.

I wipe my eyes and think about what Buck said about leg irons that masters put around their slaves. The smaller the band, the more the master trusts his slave. I think about what Buck said about the ring that Pa wears. That ring was Grandpa's and now Pa wears it, and for better or worse, it reminds him every day of his Pa and all that we were before the war.

I think of how we all eventually become captive to somebody or some thing. Buck was a slave to Pa, and in Pa's mind he still is. Tempy was a slave to the Confederates, and in his own mind Grandpa was a slave to us, even though he went and freed himself for himself, without thinking about anyone but himself.

Before the war, Pa was a big, strong, proud man who liked Henry more than me. I never saw Pa ask for anything, and I never saw Pa cry. Pa is different now, and so am I, and so is Buck, and so is Brother Davenport, and it is all because of the war, and because of this time when we are just trying to survive.

Brother Davenport wipes his face with his handkerchief

and gets to work straightaway. He gives us five bushels of corn. Then he tells me and Buck to drive the wagon through the garden to the smokehouse. He swings open the smokehouse door and gives us a side of meat. He brings it out himself and throws it in the wagon, where it lands with a *thud*.

Pa looks at all the bounty in his wagon.

"Parson, if we ever get able, I will repay you for it."

"All right, Mr. Russell, if you do or if you don't. It's all right."

We three go home rejoicing. Tonight we will have smoked meat, and Ma will make cornbread. Pa will tell us about the worms that floated up from his hardtack whenever he dipped it into his coffee, and he will say that after a while he got so hungry he drank the coffee and ate the hardtack, worms and all. He will tell us this story with a laugh now, because there is food on the table.

Sitting next to Pa in the wagon, I watch him laugh as heartily as he has just cried. Maybe Pa cried because he knew that he would have used that army rifle on his neighbor just to get a little corn for his family, and maybe he didn't like knowing that he would have done this. Maybe Brother Davenport cried for the same reason. But they both cried for what looked to be a lot of reasons, not just one.

"Oh, bloody hell, it's good to be alive," Pa says. My side is pushing against his side, my leg is knocking against his. I have never heard my father swear, and for a moment I know what it must have been like to be Henry. I think of how they must have laughed and cursed as they marched together toward a battlefield.

Within a month's time Pa regains his strength and hires out to Mr. MacLaurin, who loans us horses and a wagon. Buck and I plow and make a crop, and in it is a little bale of cotton that ends up weighing three hundred pounds. We sell that cotton for fifty cents a pound in gold, and then we go and repay Brother Davenport for his meat and corn.

XII

Spring 1863

BUCK IS HAVING TROUBLE READING out loud to Bit, and Bit doesn't like it one bit. Buck's reading voice keeps Bit from crying while a tooth is coming in, but Buck says he can't see the words so good and he has headaches. Bit cries and keeps us all up for the third night in a row.

At breakfast, Ma says there is nothing in the world wrong with Buck that a good pair of spectacles can't cure. There is a store near the Floyd Hotel, and Ma says surely they have a pair of spectacles.

"There's too much work to do," Pa says.

"Bit wouldn't be here if it weren't for Buck," Ma says.

Buck and I stare at the counter with a few already made shirts and pants next to a jar of pickled eggs ready for eating. There are no shoes. Shoes go to soldiers.

Pa greets Mr. Cook, who stands behind the counter and goes on and on about how he doesn't have any corn to sell. Mr. Cook's partner disappeared a week ago while on a trip to New Orleans to buy goods for the store. Everybody in town is saying how he was ambushed by Yankees or a band of escaped Negroes.

"Could've been our own men, too," Pa says to Mr. Cook, lighting his pipe with his one hand. "They're still out there looking for anybody with a suspicious amount of food or money."

"I suppose," Mr. Cook says. He wears a gray shirt shot through with several holes. The shirt looks as though it was once white, and I think it is surely a dead soldier's shirt. I wonder how he can stand to wear it.

Our troops show no sign of giving up anytime soon. Mr. Lincoln has recently issued something called the Emancipation Proclamation, which says all slaves in the South are free. Everybody in the county is ignoring the proclamation, because it comes from Mr. Lincoln, president of the Yankees, and they don't count.

"Mr. Cook, we come for a pair of spectacles and some matches," Pa says.

"You gettin' too old to shoot straight, Jack?" Mr. Cook sets a pair of spectacles on the counter.

"Buck, come try these out," Pa says.

Mr. Cook picks up the spectacles and puts them back in the drawer.

"Here y'matches." He brings out a box of matches. "We're all out of specs."

"You oughta know better'n that, Jack." A man's voice comes from out of the corner. I hadn't noticed Bilbo Smith sitting there in his Confederate uniform. Word is that his wife, Tid, is expecting to have a baby and Bilbo's home on furlough. He spends a good part of his time in the store with Mr. Cook, playing poker and pall-mall. "You must have it bad."

"Have what?" Pa says, smoke coming out of his mouth. "What've I got, Bilbo?"

"Nigger love."

"Soon you'll be wantin' them to vote," Mr. Cook says. "Ain't that right, Bilbo? As if the Negro could comprehend the political situations of these devastating times." Mr. Cook grumbles and laughs. I think for a moment that he has gone crazy with too much war. Three of his sons died at the Battle of Corinth, and his wife got the fever and passed last fall. Ever since the railroad shut down, he's had trouble getting anything for the store. He looks all around, then busies himself with a few empty boxes.

Pa puts some money on the counter for the matches and we set out to leave.

"Thought I heard someone coming round our house late last night," Mr. Smith says. He looks at Buck and leans further down into his chair. "Yep. I known it. I heard a body splashin' through the river that runs past our property line. Jack? Where was your boy?"

"Shanks?" Pa says. "Shanks is asleep before you can blow out the candles."

"Not Shanks. Yer nigger boy there."

Pa looks over at Buck. "I don't check up on Buck after a working day."

Mr. Smith smiles and looks around the room, as if the jar of pickled eggs and the shirts and trousers are a jury in his very own courtroom. "I think we've found the boy who's been trespassing on my property. And I do believe he might be the very same boy who's been thieving your corn, Mr. Cook."

"Ain't got no corn," Mr. Cook starts. "I done told you that, Bilbo. Haven't had corn now for—"

"And the reason you don't got none, Charlie, is 'cause this here nigger boy's been taking it all."

Mr. Cook looks at Buck as though he's got himself an idea.

"Buck goes to his house after supper," I say, stepping forward. Pa turns and looks at me like I am some mouse that just started talking.

"Shanks," Pa says, shaking his head.

"Every night," I go on, "Buck eats his dinner, then he goes on to his shack to sleep. And besides, Buck couldn't have been in your stream, Mr. Smith. He's got hydrophoby."

"Hide a what?" Mr. Smith asks.

I am pleased to be telling Mr. Smith about something he doesn't know. "Buck's scared of water."

On our way home, Buck and Pa aren't saying much of anything, but I can't stop talking about all that was in the store, and how angry in general Mr. Smith seems.

"Why is he so angry, Pa?"

"War does that to a fellow," Pa says. "That and he knows he's gotta go back. It's working on him."

"But it should make him happy, seeing how Tid's expecting a baby and all. And all he does is go to Mr. Cook's and try to stir up trouble."

"Could be that Tid's condition is making him angrier, as this is his first leave in over a year. And it's hard to accept the prospect of bringing up a child in a world such as this."

"You were happy to see Bit, though. Weren't you?"

"Yes. Yes, I was."

"I sure told him though, huh, Pa? Huh, Buck?" I look in the back of the wagon, where Buck is riding. I can't see his face.

There aren't many Negroes left in Smith County. Most of them have gone to Saint Louis or Chicago.

"Seems to me folks should be real glad for the colored people like Buck who stay here just because they want to," I say. Pa keeps his eyes on the road and doesn't say anything.

"Seems to me little boys should mind they own bidness." Pa tells Ben to giddyup.

We see the boy hanging from a tree. There are men and women, white and black, standing around, looking up at his lifeless body. He hangs from one of the prettiest live oaks in Smith County. There are notes pinned on him, not to his clothes but to the skin of his chest. When we get closer and I see his open, bugged eyes and his swollen gray-blue tongue,

I jump down from the wagon and retch in the bushes. The hanging body is little Martin, the slave boy from Irene Beall's plantation.

All around me people are talking about how Martin had set out in the night, to walk toward the Mississippi River and freedom.

Pa is yelling for me to get back in the wagon. I cannot make out what the notes say on the boy's chest. Pa slows the wagon to a stop and I get back in. I sit in the back with Buck.

"Buck?"

He is staring at the hanging boy and at the people looking up at the hanging boy. I hold on to his arm, glad to feel the living warmth of it. As we pass, we look at the crowd around the hanging boy. Have they always been this way? Our neighbors? So angry? Is it the war that made them turn animal? Is the hanging boy like slavery—something to get used to?

I feel heartsick at the sight of that boy, and I'd like to kill any person who done such a thing, but that don't seem right either, to kill a man for killing, especially if killing is what got you fired up. I remember how tired Tempy was with killing, but then that was war. This was just murder.

"Pa?" I cannot think of the question that I mean to ask.

"It's gettin' late, boys. Yer ma's probably gettin' worried."

XIII

Summer 1863

I WAKE UP TO THE SOUND of shattering glass. I hear men's voices outside. Angry voices. It must be almost midnight.

"Pa?"

Ma and Pa are already out on the porch. Ma has a shawl wrapped around her shoulders and over Bit. Pa has his rifle.

Two men sit on horseback outside of Buck's shack. Each of them has a torch and a rifle. They are yelling for Buck to come out. One of them turns toward us, and I see that it is Mr. Cook.

"Bilbo? Charlie?" Pa says. "You fellows best be going."

"You stay out of this, Jack." I can't see his face, but I know that's Mr. Smith talking. I have not heard his voice since that day at the store in the spring. Is Mr. Smith home on furlough again, or is he a deserter like Tempy? It is July 4, and nobody celebrated because Vicksburg has just fallen.

Buck comes out, head up.

"Take yer hands out of yer pockets, boy."

Buck puts his hands in the air. He doesn't say anything, and that gets my goat. I want to yell at these men. I want to yank them down off their horses and say, *Now get,* and I want Pa to do the same.

"You're on my property," Pa says.

The men point their guns at us. They wouldn't have done this three years ago, before the war. They wouldn't have had the guns.

I feel Ma's arm around me and I think, quit bothering with *me,* somebody should be putting an arm around Buck.

One of the men gets down off his horse and takes hold of Buck, and I step forward, out of Ma's reach. I feel Pa's hand on my shoulder.

"But Pa." I whisper and I am ashamed that I am whispering on the porch of my own home. "They mean to do Buck harm."

"Shanks, you listen to your pa," Ma says.

"What you fixin' to do with Buck?" Pa says.

"This here boy's not yer property no more, Jack."

Mr. Cook laughs. "That's right. Emancipation Proclamation."

"No, Charlie," Mr. Smith says. "It's the Fourth of July. Independence Day."

I take a step forward, but Ma holds tight.

"Now run, boy." Mr. Smith points his gun at Buck's head. Buck steps off his porch and heads toward the open road.

"Not that way," Mr. Smith says. "That way."

They lead him into the woods behind his shack.

Mr. Smith sets out after Buck. "We're fixin' to set you free."

Pa goes inside the house and puts his gun away. I follow him.

"We gotta go after them, Pa. You seen what they did to that boy outside of town. They strung him up and hanged him. We gotta save Buck."

Pa shakes his head. "We can't get back Buck, any more than we can get back Henry." He lies down in his bed and stares at the ceiling.

Ma goes white.

"You're wrong," I say, feeling like I just cursed at my own Pa. Ma looks at me like I'm in her dream.

I get Pa's rifle and minnie balls from under his bed. Ma just stares at me wide-eyed.

"Jack?" she says as I go out the front door.

They aren't hard to find, and I know those woods better than they do. They are down by the Leaf River, and when I catch up to them, one of them has Buck kneeling in the water.

"Understand you scared of water, boy," I overhear him say. I can't hear well enough to know if Buck says anything back. I expect he doesn't, but something gets the man riled up enough to dunk Buck's head underwater. I can hear the splash. I can't make it all out in the dark, but I hear a gasp and I guess that the man brings Buck's head up again. The man says something I can't hear.

I think the voice belongs to Mr. Smith, and Mr. Cook is standing behind them. Their horses are tethered to a tree.

Mr. Cook hollers something, and as he hollers I cock my rifle. All of a sudden they turn and aim their guns at me. I hold my breath and don't move. I'm sure they heard the *click* of Pa's rifle.

I have every right to pull the trigger, but I can't get my

finger to squeeze. I can't. I think of that boy, Martin, whom we saw hanging from the tree outside town. I think how Martin could have been Buck, might be Buck. I make myself hate hate hate Mr. Smith and Mr. Cook. But still I can't squeeze.

I don't know who will die first, but I hope it's me. This is all my fault. I told Mr. Smith what all Buck did every night, so he knew just when to come. Worst of all, I told him Buck's deepest fear, his fear of water. I might as well have loaded his gun.

"Hey Jack, hope yer not comin' after this here nigger boy," one of the men says to Pa, who has emerged from the woods behind me. Mr. Smith and Mr. Cook have their guns aimed at Pa as he saunters toward them like he's out taking an evening constitutional.

"Ah, come on now Bilbo, Charlie. Haven't you had about enough of that?" Pa walks right up to their gun barrels. He's talking, but I can't hear what he's saying now.

I can't hear anything. I cup my earlobes with my hands. All I catch is "Set him loose" and "bloodiness."

Buck is still at the riverbank. He is on all fours and I can't see his face in this dark. From this distance, it could be that they are all at a baptism and Buck's just there praying.

I bring the gun up and aim, but Pa is in my line of fire.

"Buck, come on over here," Pa says.

But Buck is frozen with fear.

"Steady," Pa says.

Buck still doesn't move.

"Shanks."

I jump at the sound of my name.

"Come over here and give Buck a hand," Pa says.

I do as I'm told. All I have to do is stand next to Buck and say his name and he stands. His clothes are dripping and his shoes make a slapping sound as he walks slowly out of the water.

"Bilbo, Charlie," Pa says in a voice he uses sometimes when he talks to Ma. "This here war'll be over soon enough, buddies."

Mr. Smith looks at Pa and prepares to say something but does not. He lowers his gun, then Mr. Cook does the same. I walk past them both, and for a moment Mr. Smith and I are about eye to eye.

"You," he says to me. I can smell the sour odor of whiskey on his breath, and he looks more muddy and worn out than angry. "You stayed behind, didn't you? Yer Pa and me, we fought for the likes of you." He is shaking his head and laughing.

I can feel the weight of Pa's hand on my shoulder. As he and I and Buck head back into the woods, we hear Mr. Smith calling out Tid's name.

Pa tells Buck he thinks there's a good chance Mr. Smith or Mr. Cook will come back.

"And if it's not them, there's going to be others. Best thing for you to do now, Buck, is leave. I don't want you to, and I know Mrs. Russell and Bit and Shanks sure don't want you to either. But we'd rather you were alive than dead."

There's blood coming from a cut over Buck's right eye, and his lower lip is swelling and bleeding, too.

"Ma can tend to those cuts and you can collect your things," I say.

"That's the first place they'll look," Pa says.

"But Pa." Everything is happening too fast. "Buck's got to go back and say goodbye to Ma. And she's most likely worried where we all are."

"This was partly yer ma's idea, son. I told her we might be gone a while."

"But Buck's got his Bible to get." I stop to think of what-all else Buck has that he needs. "You already have yer madstone, right?"

"We could go back and you could take the mule, Buck," Pa says. "You'll get farther."

"Much obliged, Mr. Jack, sir, but I don't think folks would look kindly on a black man riding a white man's mule." Buck's voice is quiet and low. "You take my Bible, Mr. Shanks. I already give that Choctaw madstone to Mr. Tempy a ways back."

I stare at Pa and then at Buck. "You mean to say you didn't have your stone with you in that water back there, Buck?"

"No, sir," Buck says. "I had this here ark." Buck reaches into his pocket and pulls out the poorly whittled boat I gave him for Christmas. We look at each other and we both smile.

"Come on," Pa says. "I don't want to leave yer ma alone for too long. We'll walk you as far as the river Strong."

We set to walking. Pa takes a long route he says is safer. We keep walking until we get tired. Then we sleep an hour, get up, and walk again. We pass through Mize. Pa walks like he knows this country as well as he knows his own farmland. Even though he walks slower with his limp, Pa leads the way, and we walk so far and it gets so late it feels like we are walking to the edge of the world.

The war is not over, and even though most of the fighting

is going on up north, we hear distant gunfire and cannon fire that sound like the drums of a far-off marching band. Most of Mississippi has been taken by the Federals, and Pa says we don't want to be mistaken for spies. Lucky for us, spies wouldn't likely be traveling with a Negro.

There are no birds nor animal sounds. It's as though the natural world has stopped altogether, waiting for the war to be over before starting up again. We pass the burned-down plantations, the blank cotton fields, and the empty slave houses. We pass a field where the air is rank, and Pa stops to look. He tells us he heard tell of a skirmish that took place here that amounted to nothing. Spring rains washed open the shallow graves, and now the bones and bits of both gray and blue uniforms are scattered all across the ground.

"Load and shoot, load and shoot," Pa says. "That's all they tell a fellow on the battlefield."

He starts walking, then stops again.

"All that fighting and all I remember seeing are eyes and teeth and open mouths shouting, and in the end all that red blood on the ground and the yellow sun, rising or setting, who knew?"

The dead are all around us. I can feel their empty stares, and I think I hear whispering. Was there a time without war?

I can't remember. I grip Pa's rifle. I forget why I ever wanted a rifle in the first place.

We walk on, and after a while we are walking in our sleep. Buck and I are both surprised when Pa says, "We're here."

"Where?" I look around and see a river I don't recognize. The sun is just coming up.

"This here's the Strong," Pa tells us.

"I thought it'd be bigger," I say.

"Heard tell of it, but never seen it before," Buck says.

"It joins up with the Pearl right over yonder," Pa says. "Buck, you cross the river here. Don't go into Jackson. Just head for the Natchez Trace. Don't take it, just cross it. Then head on to the Mississippi River. Avoid the roads. Sleep during the day, travel at night. Make fires with oak bark, 'cause it don't give off much smoke. You can get a boat on the Mississippi that will take you as far north as you want to go. You'll pass Vicksburg along your way." He reaches into his pocket.

"Here's money for those spectacles. These here are wages you earned fair and square." Pa hands Buck a piece of paper with writing on it. "I don't know what this says. They give it to me when I bought you. I think yer ma and pa's name is on there."

"These here are my freedom papers," Buck says, looking

down at the writing. Once a man possesses his own freedom papers, he's free. I am glad now that Buck can read it all.

When Pa shakes Buck's hand, I know I am not ready to say goodbye.

"I'll cross with you," I say.

"I'll be all right," Buck says. We stand facing each other. We are the same height now.

"Can I go with him, Pa?" For a moment I can picture the two of us crossing rivers and twisted railroads, passing the ruins of Vicksburg, running across battlegrounds of the newly dead, dodging bullets and cannon fire.

"We need you here." I can tell from the sound of Pa's voice that he thought about letting me go.

"You'll be all right," Buck says. He looks straight at me, right into my eyes. No black man with a master looks into anybody's eyes. And then he does the darnedest thing. He hugs me. I can smell his spicy sweat, and I don't want him to let go.

But he does.

Pa and I watch Buck as he crosses the river. He doesn't freeze up. He doesn't even hesitate. He wades right on through, holding his head high, and we wave when he gets to the other side. Then he disappears into the woods.

"It sure would be somethin'," I say. "Gettin' on a flatboat, maybe a steamboat, goin' to a whole new country."

"We'll all be one country again soon enough," Pa says.

We both look out at the water.

Buck didn't even leave with his madstone. He doesn't need it anymore. I finger the arrowhead in my pocket. Grandpa said it would make me strong, but it never did me any good at all.

"Maybe Buck'll come back someday."

"Maybe."

I throw the arrowhead out over the water. It lands with a *smack* and skips the surface three times.

We round up some hickory branches and carve them into spears. After a while, we spear two good-sized fish. We make a fire out of oak bark with the matches Pa has, and we cook the fish over the sticks. After we eat, we rest on the riverbank.

The yellow jackets are out, and a Maypop tree drops old red maypops, which float and bobble on the river as they are slowly carried away by the current. We can both smell the warm, wormy air.

"Tell me about how Henry died, Pa."

For a while Pa doesn't respond, but then he sighs long

and deep. He takes off his shoes and puts his bare feet in the river. I don't recollect seeing Pa's bare feet before. They are long and thin and paler than white.

"We managed to stay together for quite some time," he starts. "In Kentucky, we had to kill a horse to eat. We cooked the meat and wrapped our feet in the hide. You know how Henry took to horses. Well, he didn't want any part of it, but his feet were getting cut by the ice. I told him the horsehair would feel good on his soles. He put them hides on finally, and I was glad for that." Pa leans back on his elbows. I hear him swallow and I wait for more.

"He got three fingers shot off in a battle in Mill Springs, Kentucky, and I was glad for that, too, thinking maybe then he could get a furlough and go home. They took him to White Hospital. I got permission to go with him. I thought I would get to stay with him, but we left the next day." Pa leans all the way back and lies down. His hair spreads out like white snow over the grass. "He caught pneumonia. He died in Bowling Green. I wasn't there."

I lean back and lie down side by side with Pa, just the way Henry and I used to sleep. I think of Henry lying sick in a hospital bed, his hand aching. Folks say when a soldier dies he dies for his country, but I don't think Henry was thinking about Mississippi or the South or the North or any of that while he lay there all alone, weak and in pain. Still, I wonder: Did he think of Pa or Ma while he coughed and bled? Did he think of me?

Used to be all I wanted was to grow up to be like Henry, have a uniform and shoes like Henry's, own a gun like Henry's, be Pa's favorite like Henry. Now Henry is dead and I am Pa's only surviving son, and I know now that my ball and chain is always going to be the memory of my older brother, Henry.

"Now you know," Pa says.

I try to speak but my throat is choked up.

I wonder if maggots got to Henry the way they got to that soldier at the schoolhouse. I wonder if maggots got to Jesus' wounds; but no, Jesus was God. No kind of bug, not even a mosquito or a no-see-um, gets on God. But Ma says Jesus was a man, after all, but only for a little while, only while he joined us on earth. So I imagine the maggots all fell away and Jesus' wounds closed back up when he quit being just another dead man and rose up from earth and on into heaven.

Surely Jesus' pa couldn't bear to see his only son suffer and deteriorate right before his very eyes. That's probably why he took him back up to heaven, so he could be with him again and the maggots wouldn't get after him. He missed him, after all. What a bright reunion they must have had!

"You all right?" I feel Pa's hand on my stomach.

"I'm all right." My voice sounds strange to me.

We both listen to the water for a while.

"It's a pretty little river, ain't it?" Pa says.

Another river, other than the Leaf or the Pearl or the Tallahala, is a wonder to me. I think of Grandpa and now I think I understand why he had the urge to keep moving, to see more.

"You did good back there in the woods with Mr. Smith and Mr. Cook," Pa says. "You would've made a fine soldier."

I look to where Pa's rifle is, up against a tree where I left it. I never fired a shot.

I take my shoes off and then lie back down next to Pa, our feet soaking in the waters of the Strong.

XIV

Summer Skirmish 1863

I WAKE UP HEARING a man talking like no other man I ever heard before. He sounds like he's talking through his nose; his words are pointy and carved.

I am no longer at the edge of the Strong but up on the bank, farther from the water's edge. Pa is down on one knee behind a bush, holding his gun in his one hand, and aiming in the direction of the voices. He makes his mouth look like it's saying *Shh*. I crawl over and kneel next to him.

Two Yankee soldiers fill their canteens at the edge of the river. We hear gunfire close by in the woods behind us. The soldiers look dirty and worn out, and even from where I am I can smell them. They smell like something burning. Their faces are caked with grease, mud, and blood. Their uniforms are so dirty and faded they could be anybody—Mr. Cook, Mr. Smith, even Pa—but their voices give them away.

They drink long and quick, then get up and head back into the woods.

"Skirmish up yonder," Pa says. I see a wildness in his eyes, like his whole face is on fire. He lowers his gun. "We're going to have to make our way back real careful like." He hands me his gun. "I'm no good with one hand, so you're gonna have to take over from here. I know you know how to load, can you shoot?"

"Yes, sir." I can tell he doesn't feel right without his gun.

"Good. Now get ready."

Pa tells me to keep as low to the ground as I can, even when we walk. We stay hunched down, and we pass a soldier, a Yankee who looks to be napping, leaning against a tree. He has a mess on his lap that looks like sausages.

"'Testines," Pa whispers and pushes me past.

The empty, dead field we passed through before is now alive with fighting. We stay close to the tree trunks and roots, and I can smell the fungus and rot. I try to get that soldier's intestines out of my mind. This is where I thought I wanted to be all along, and it's true I can't keep my eyes off the fighting. There is so much smoke from the gunfire it's hard to see, but I hear all the moaning from the wounded.

"We wanna head for the tracks," Pa says. "You know your way."

Fog rolls down on us and I can't tell if this is good or bad. The soldiers can't see us, so we can sneak by, but we can't see them either, and we may sneak right into their line of fire.

I hear the minnie balls whizzing right past, too close to my ears. I can't see but two feet in front of me, and the moaning and hollering sounds ghostly.

Just then a soldier runs toward us, and he is just as surprised to see us as we are him. I can't tell if he's Confederate or Federal, and before either he or I can aim and shoot, he comes charging at Pa with his bayonet. He takes one clean swipe at him and I hear Pa scream. I fire and my bullet hits that soldier man in the back. I watch him fall away from Pa. I get a look at his uniform and realize he was one of our own. And I killed him. I killed one of our own.

I have only killed rabbits for eating, and the one deer I shot, Grandpa helped me with. That deer kept us well fed for a whole winter. Now I have killed a man, and I know it was right, but it still don't feel right. I wonder what God has planned for me and all the soldiers who kill. I can no longer imagine sitting down to supper with the likes of Grandma behind Saint Peter's gates. I'd be better off at a mess table with all the rest of them.

Soldiers are retreating, or just moving on to somewhere else—I can't tell which, only that they are moving away from us, and there's less and less gunfire and more and more moaning. Pa's hurt bad and he stops me when I try to move him. I put my face close to his so he can tell me what to do. He stares straight up at the sky, except you can't see the sky for all the fog, and only when I move my face close to his chest do I see through all the blood, so much blood, that he's cut bad.

"Oh God, Pa. Oh God."

I can see inside Pa. A red muscle in his chest throbs. Surely it is Pa's heart that I see, and I am filled with wonder and horror.

"Don't bury me." He speaks with every breath. "Just leave me. You get along now. Go home. Tell yer ma I love her. Take care of her and Bit. I love you, son." Pa's face is white. "We done some good. That's all."

I'm watching the life run out of him and I want to scream

out, "Oh no, Pa. No." I lie down next to him, trying to rally him. This is not anything like when Grandma died and I wanted to run from the house. This is Pa, and I don't want to let the maggots get to him. I don't want Pa to die.

With my head down, I shimmy over to the dead soldier. I tell him I'm sorry for killing him, sorry too for what I am about to do. I take the canteen from around his neck and rummage through his knapsack.

The dead soldier has a spare shirt and a roll of bandages, all of which I tie tight around Pa's chest, and the bleeding seems to slow down some. I lift Pa's head and he drinks the water from the dead man's canteen.

"You're gonna be all right, Pa. You're gonna make it. Now we need to get you up from here and get over to those tracks. We can rest some there."

Pa's looking at me but he's not moving.

"We've got to get home to Ma. I know you told her we'd be gone a while, but this here's been a too long while."

Finally, with his hand on his chest, Pa gets up and leans on me. The fog is still rolling in, and I am glad for it now because it keeps them from seeing us and it keeps me from seeing all the dead men I know are scattered all around us. We keep ourselves as low as the fog, and any time we almost step on a dead man, I try not to look, and I don't say a thing. We just zigzag our way across that field, slow like, and after a while we make our way to the railroad tracks.

The tracks are pulled up, and one of the rails is twisted around a tree. We crouch under it. Pa drinks more water while I watch the Yankees burn a bridge with the railway cars still on it. I can see the hot fires inside the cars, and even as they fall, it does not look real. More like a toy train set. None of it looks real. Nothing feels real. The soldiers yell and holler and keep tearing up and burning everything in sight. These soldiers look like a pack of spoiled children who've gone and ruined a game.

"We need to get back home to Ma," I say.

"Ma," Pa says.

Pa is weak, but if we stay here he might fall asleep and die. I don't want him to rest, because I don't want him to sleep.

"Pa. See that bank of trees over yonder? Let's us try and make it there."

Pa nods. "Get us home, son."

We use the twisted tracks for cover and make our way over to the bank of trees; before we can settle there for long, I point out another set of trees to Pa.

We do this over and over, and we both know it is like a

game, but we don't admit it. We find a target and we get to it, only to find another target, then another, and another.

Our house looks different. It is gray, and it's like I notice for the first time that it needs whitewashing, but I know now that this house is never going to look the same to me. Pa picks up the pace when he sees Ma standing there on the porch, and for a moment I think of what Ma sees coming down the road—her husband and her son. Surely she thinks this is the way it should have been when Pa first came home from the war. Surely she thinks I should not be me. I should be her first son, Henry, and I feel bad just then, bad for being me.

Ma is holding fast to Pa and they are both smiling and crying and then so am I.

"I thought I'd lost you both," Ma says.

Pa is leaning heavy on Ma as we help him up the steps to the porch. Brother Davenport is there, and so is Mrs. Davenport, who is smiling and holding Bit.

We get Pa inside and lay him down on the feather bed, and Ma sets to work on his wounds. The dead soldier's shirt and bandages that I wrapped around Pa's chest are brown now with Pa's dried blood. Mrs. Davenport plops Bit beside Brother Davenport and gets to cooking at the stove. Bit reaches up and squeezes Brother Davenport's nose, and he looks like he's trying to like it.

Ma gives me clean clothes to change into, and I wash up in the kitchen. I am too excited and too amazed that I'm alive, to be tired. Mrs. Davenport tells me word got out that Pa and me walked Buck to freedom and so she and Brother Davenport came to look after Ma. It took Pa and me so long to return, she says, that they thought the worst, and already some folks have come around, bringing over their best sympathy dishes. Mrs. Davenport points out the mashed sweet potatoes on the table. Then I remember: I am hungry.

We hear a knock at the door, and there stands Irene Beall holding a pecan pie. Her eyes and nose are red and puffy from crying. She looks around the room. Ma stands smiling in the doorway with Pa, who is wearing a fresh bandage around his chest and a clean shirt. Little Bit has grabbed hold of Brother Davenport's nose again, and now they're both laughing. I am wearing Henry's old Sunday clothes.

"I thought you and your pa were dead," Irene says, sniffing.

"Well don't be sore that we're not," I say.

Irene bites her bottom lip and walks right on up to me, looking so hard and so mean I think surely she will slap me.

She sets down her pie, and then she does the oddest thing. She leans forward and kisses me, smack, right there on my right cheek in front of everyone, and I know that I am turning red as oxblood.

"Come on," Mrs. Davenport says. "My chicken's getting cold."

We all of us sit down at the table and eat chicken, mustard greens, black-eyed peas, cornbread, sweet potatoes, and Irene's pecan pie. I eat so much I sweat, and then I eat a little more.

"Mr. Russell," Brother Davenport says, pushing his chair away from the table. "I have to tell you what I think."

We all prepare ourselves to listen.

"You did a fine thing. You got people talking and thinking about their own slaves. Everybody around here knows you and they respect you. You never did a thing wrong. Your family has never once been in trouble with the law. You all have always played by the rules. Now you've up and freed your own slave and given him his life back. Took a brave man to do that, Mr. Russell. A brave man."

We lift our chipped water cups and toast Pa.

"I wish you'd been there when those men chased down

our poor Martin," Irene says. "He wasn't but thirteen years old. Ever since then, ever since they hung him, I've thought of what all I didn't do to stop them."

Pa puts a napkin to his mouth. "Miss Irene, Brother Davenport. I would love to take all the credit, but freeing Buck was all my son's doing." Everybody turns and looks at me. "He made me take a hard look at Buck's situation. He did the right thing and that made me do the right thing."

I surely never seen a smile like the one on Irene's face, not even that time when she was helping the sick soldiers; and for just a time, it feels like the war is finally over and none of us have lost.

"'Sides that, he saved my life," Pa says. "You should've seen him out there. I'd be dead on the ground if it weren't for Shanks."

Ma, she reaches across the table and holds my hand and says, "Frank," and I know that's my name from here on out. I have to close my eyes for a minute because I keep seeing so much—too much—but even with my eyes shut I see it all, like when you shut your eyes in the dark and you see white light. I can still see the burning coals inside the train cars, the maggots on the dead soldier's arm, the chains around Tempy's ankles, the pennies over Grandma's eyes, the cut on

Buck's brow, the noose around Martin's neck, the Yankee with the lap full of intestines. And I can't get Pa out of my eyesight. There is always going to be Pa there, spread out and torn apart, his heart laid open to me.

Still, I am back, back home, and nothing, none of it, looks the same or feels the same, and I guess that is because I am not Shanks anymore. I am Frank.

Epilogue

THE WAR effectively ends on April 9, 1865, at Appomattox, Virginia. In 1866, one fifth of our state's entire budget goes to artificial limbs. In 1869, Mississippi adopts a new state constitution which says the Negro cannot vote. In 1870, our state is readmitted into the union, as if it were never admitted in 1817. Also in 1870, a private school opens for white girls and boys only, and Robert E. Lee dies.

Grandpa never does come back, and we never do hear another word about him.

I miss Buck. He writes to us once, and Ma reads the letter

out loud to Pa and me and Bit at the noonday meal, then gives the letter to me, and I go sit under the two pines shaped like a Y and read it over again to myself. He made it as far north as Chicago, working on the railroads. He witnessed the great fire that destroyed most of the city in October of 1871. Still, like Ma always said, he felt he was lucky to be alive. He took a train east on tracks that he had helped build. He's in New York now, wearing his new spectacles, helping to build a bridge that will link the great cities of Brooklyn and New York.

When I fold Buck's letter back up, I lean against the trunk of the two pines that have become one tree. Lightning was what done it. That's what Grandpa said. Sometimes it's the one mighty outburst that leads to something altogether different, sometimes good, sometimes bad. Buck was scared of water and then Mr. Smith tried to drown him. Now Buck is fearless, suspended high over a body of water called the East River, building the biggest bridge there ever was.

Lightning hit that tree and killed a part of it, but not all of it. With Henry and so many others dead seems like the war has done the same to Pa and Ma and me, even the likes of Mr. Smith. Ma *was* right: we are lucky because we are alive. But for better or worse, a part of all of us is dead.

Our country fell apart, and for a time so did we. But some of us are still left, and we are strong enough to put ourselves and our world back together.

I talk to Brother Davenport a good deal. He's got me teaching little children up at the public schoolhouse. As much as we talk, I still don't know why God went and put that tree in the garden, or why he chose to pit the North and the South against each other and cause so much death and heartache.

Seems like it takes a lot to know a little about God. You got to know what kind of roots to dig to brew teas that heal what ails you, and you got to know how to read so you can learn what all happened before you were ever born. You got to know what to do while you're living, but you also got to know about burying people, and saying goodbye. You got to know about the living, and you got to know about the dying part, too. Jesus did. And so did his pa.

These days, everything new begins to happen at once in Smith County. George Anderson operates his first telegraph station in Taylorsville. Mr. Childre, who made shoes for all the soldiers, buys the old Floyd Hotel, installs a telephone, and writes up his bills on a fancy machine called a typewriter.

Pa keeps his gun under his bed, but we'll never use it again. Ma bakes cakes and pies and sells them for a good profit. People know her best for her peach and apple pies. Between Ma's baking and my teaching and Pa's harvests, we save enough money each year to buy more land to farm. Pa and I are building a house on a parcel of land that will soon be my very own, and I have my own plans for it.

One spring day Brother Davenport gets word that there is going to be an old sacred harp singing convention. He says a group of men advertised that they would be at the sing and would come by way of bicycle. A bicycle is something that no one has ever heard of. The following Sunday, we all set out for the Calvary Church just a few miles south of Mize.

We pass the live oak where Pa, Buck, and I saw the hanging colored boy named Martin. I look at that tree now and I hate that I hate such a pretty tree for having had a part in hanging that little boy.

We pass the Gulf and Ship Island Railroad that is finally built and running. There is no sign of Sherman neckties, the tracks those soldiers had burned and twisted into bow shapes.

More people show up at the Calvary Church than I ever recall seeing, even before the war. The Dutch family who settled in the county about the same time we did are there with their grown children and new twin babies. It being an occasion, Mr. McCollum is wearing his white linen trousers from Scotland. They hang off his skinny frame, but he still gets the young ladies to come examine the horn buttons that fasten on the side.

I see Irene and her ma putting flowers on the family graves by the side of the church. The sons who were younger than I was had gone off to fight the last year of the war and none of them came back alive. Irene is the last of the Bealls.

This feeling I have toward Irene is nothing like what I felt that first time I went sparking at her place. Nowadays just a glimpse of her yellow hair can stop my heart, then make me go calm all at once. I have talked to Pa and Ma, and I have made up my mind. When Irene and her ma return from the cemetery, I will go to Mrs. Beall and make my intentions clear. I will say, "Mrs. Beall, you know how I feel about your daughter. Already I am twenty years old, and I will soon have my own house and my own land. I have my business arranged so that I can make my plans known."

Ma sets up a table and spreads out her cakes and pies to sell, while Pa shows off Bit, who is wearing a new, store-bought dress and is playing with my new little brother, Jack, who is named after Pa.

The sheriff stops and buys a peach pie from Ma. He tells us he just got word that Tempy never did get back to Missouri, and he didn't get caught again either. Last they heard, Tempy was with a company of deserters numbering about three hundred in Jones County. Some of them went on to Honey Island, Louisiana, and others went as far as New Orleans, where Tempy signed up as a Union soldier.

Tid Smith is near the picnic tables, play-wrestling with her husband, who is using his one leg to push her away. He lost a leg at the Battle of Tupelo in Pontotoc County. Word is he dresses up in white sheets at night and rides around scaring the Negroes all in the name of a secret society named the Ku Klux Klan. The Smiths' little boy is playing marbles in the dirt. Folks who pass by make discreet comments about the child's teeny-tiny head and his halo of peculiar red hair.

At about ten o'clock, the singing stops and we look up the road at two men who are pedaling their bicycles at a rapid speed of at least three or four miles an hour. They are in their shirtsleeves, and the wind has gathered in their bosoms, and they look like two balloons heading toward us. We all stand paralyzed and amazed. Are all inventions finished when such beauty comes?

At the noon hour, dinner is spread under the shade of the oak trees, and everybody eats to their satisfaction. But still we all stare at the bicycles, which are leaning against the tree trunks, and admire the blue and the steel. I wonder how such a great convenience might change our lives.

After the eating and visiting, after I talk first with Irene and then with Mrs. Beall, and our families celebrate our future, after the singing and praying, the bicycle men announce they have to return to Jackson. The churchyard fills with all of us, and none of us wants the day to end. We shout for the men to ride around the yard a few more times. They ride, and after we have studied the operations of the bicycle as best we can, they say farewell.

"Play somethin', Frank," Pa says.

I take out my harmonica, and because Irene is near me and I feel like hearing it, I play a song I recall Grandpa playing once. We all gaze as the men on bicycles ride by, their shirts billowing, and without turning around or looking back, they pedal fast down the road and into a new world.

Author's Note

I WAS BORN in Newton, Mississippi, north of Soso and west of Chunky. When I was growing up, my grandfather talked about "the war" as though it had happened yesterday. He often took me to the Mount Zion Cemetery, where there is a marker that honors two boys in our family. Myth has it that when their father went off to war and they were supposed to stay behind, these two brothers, aged fifteen and sixteen, left home and joined the cavalry. "Yankees killed them at the Battle of Murfreesboro in Tennessee," my grandfather used to tell me. I thought about those two boys so often that I felt that they were my brothers and that they had died in my lifetime. Years later my father moved us away from Mississippi, up north to Chicago. Whenever we went back to Newton to visit my grandfather, he would call us Yankees. He made us feel miserable—for leaving or for returning, I was never sure which.

My grandfather talked so much about his ancestors that his wife, my grandmother, barely got a word in about her side of the family—some of whom were Russells. Soon after my grandmother died a few years ago, a relative gave me a manuscript she had found in a shoebox while cleaning out a closet in my grandmother's house. Apparently my grandmother's great-uncle, Frank Russell, talked out his life to someone before he died, and that person wrote it all down. The manuscript, called *The Life and Times of Frank Russell*, turned out to be a wonderful rough sketch of Frank Russell's life in Smith County, Mississippi, during the 1850s and 1860s.

The part of Frank's story that interested me the most, however, was what he did *not* talk about. When the "menfolk" went off to war, Frank was left at home with the women and children. But Frank did not talk about that time, and I could not stop thinking about what being left behind must have felt like for young Frank—during a war of such high stakes—and that is how I came to shape the character of Frank Russell in my story.

The real Frank Russell really did make his own shoes, really did go sparking (though not with Irene Beall), really did pull fodder; and when his father came home from the war, they really did have to go begging for food from a neighbor, and they wept real tears. As the real Frank Russell said in his memoir, "those were devastating times."

Like his fictional counterpart, Frank Russell was indeed lucky: he survived the war and managed to pull himself and his family together and move forward into the future.

My father often talked about how rough Smith County was. After the war, Confederate soldiers brought home their guns, and for the first time most every family was armed.

I wrote this story for my son, James, who at age six is already impatient about becoming a man and growing strong.

I also wrote this story for my father. Like many southerners, my father loves the storytelling, the food, the history, and all the natural beauty of his home state of Mississippi. And like many southerners, my father also knows about *all* of the South's past and *all* that it has lost and will perhaps never regain.

I still listen to stories about General Sherman's raids through Mississippi, how women hid the family silver, and what people ate during those years of hard times. But I especially like to hear the stories about the Negroes' great migration north: what tricks they used to keep the dogs away, the songs they sang to signal their leave-taking, the secret routes they took to freedom. Buck got to Chicago, where my father took us. I don't know that Buck would ever have called himself a Yankee, but I think that, like my father, for better or worse, Buck will always have Mississippi in his heart.